mary-kate olsen   ashley olsen

so little time

Check out these other great
so little time
titles:

Book 1: **how to train a boy**

Book 2: **instant boyfriend**

Book 3: **too good to be true**

Coming soon!

Book 5: **tell me about it**

mary-kate olsen   **ashley** olsen

so little time

just between us

By Jacqueline Carrol

Based on the teleplay by Michael Baser and Frank Dungan

HarperEntertainment
An *Imprint of* HarperCollins*Publishers*

A PARACHUTE PRESS BOOK

A PARACHUTE PRESS BOOK

Parachute Publishing, L.L.C.
156 Fifth Avenue, Suite 302
New York, NY 10010

Published by
HarperEntertainment
An *Imprint of* HarperCollins*Publishers*
10 East 53rd Street, New York, NY 10022-5299

ISBN 0-06-008806-0

HarperCollins®, **, and HarperEntertainment™ are trademarks of HarperCollins Publishers Inc.

First printing: July 2002

Printed in the United States of America

Visit HarperEntertainment on the World Wide Web at
www.harpercollins.com

10 9 8 7 6 5 4 3 2 1

chapter
one

"I am *so* not in the mood for school today," Riley Carlson declared to her twin sister, Chloe.

Chloe glanced at her across the kitchen table. "Why?" she asked. "You don't have any tests, do you? And you get to see Alex."

"True," Riley agreed, munching on a piece of toast. Alex Zimmer was her boyfriend. "Unfortunately, Willow will be there, too."

"Oh. Right," Chloe said. "Willow."

"Who is this Willow person?" Manuelo asked, turning from the stove where he was cracking eggs into a pan. Manuelo Del Valle had been the Carlsons' house-keeper/cook/nanny since the girls were babies. He liked to know everything that was going on.

"Willow Sweet," Chloe told him, sipping orange juice. "She's Alex's old girlfriend. Manuelo, you're not making those eggs for me, are you?" she added.

"No, Chloe. I know you don't care for a good, fortifying breakfast," he replied. He gestured toward the other end of kitchen, where Jake and Macy Carlson were leaning against a counter, looking at swatches of material. "I'm making them for your father. Your mother asked his advice about fabrics for her new line. He'll need his strength."

[Riley: Wait a sec. Maybe I should explain the parental living situation to you. It's like this: Mom and Dad are total opposites, and they separated a few months ago. Until then, they ran a fashion design company together, and they were always fighting. Dad wanted to get back to basics, so now he lives in a trailer on the beach and practices yoga a lot. Mom is still very driven and runs the business by herself. But, believe it or not, our parents actually get along now that they don't live together. The cool thing is that we are all still really close, and Riley and I get to see our dad a lot.]

"Now, back to this Willow person," Manuelo said as the eggs sizzled. "Riley?"

Riley sighed and slipped a piece of crust to Pepper, their black and white cocker spaniel, who had stationed herself under the table. "Chloe's right. Willow used to be Alex's girlfriend. Then her family moved to London for a while."

"But now she's back," Chloe said. "And she's after Alex. Tell him what happened, Riley."

"Hold on." Manuelo tilted the eggs onto a plate and set it in front of Jake Carlson. "You don't want to use linen," he said, pointing to a swatch of pale green. "Breathe on linen and it wrinkles."

"He's right," Jake said to Macy. "You're right, Manuelo. Thanks for the eggs, by the way."

"At your service." Manuelo turned back to Riley. "Now. Tell me what happened."

"I saw one of Willow's notebooks," Riley said. "I mean, it was a total accident. There was this backpack lying around, and I was trying to find out whose it was, so I looked inside."

"And she found Willow's notebook," Chloe went on. "Willow had written Alex's name all over it!"

"But that doesn't have to mean that Willow wants him back," Manuelo said. "She could have written his name for another reason."

[**Riley: Can you think of another reason? Like maybe Willow was practicing her penmanship? Oh, sure. And after she wrote his name a thousand times, she drew pink hearts around them just for fun!**]

"Chloe didn't tell you the best part. I mean, the worst," Riley said. She told Manuelo about the hearts.

"I see your point," Manuelo admitted.

3

"I still can't believe it," Riley declared. "All this time Willow has been pretending to be nice to me. And telling Alex that she justs want to be friends with him."

"But Alex doesn't like Willow that way anymore," Chloe reminded her. "He likes *you*."

Riley smiled. She and Alex *did* have a great thing going. They didn't have to do anything special, either. Walking on the beach, getting ice cream, sitting around talking—just being together was enough.

And then there was the song. Riley's best friend, Sierra Pomeroy, had started a rock band called The Wave. Alex played guitar in it and also wrote songs. He'd actually written one especially for Riley, which was so cool.

"So what is the problem?" Manuelo asked. "If Alex likes you and not Willow, then everything is fine."

"No, it's not," Riley argued. "Alex thinks Willow is great—he doesn't have a clue she wants him back. He says he's totally over her, but I'm still a little nervous. She's *always* hanging around him."

"Plus, she's gorgeous," Chloe added.

"Don't remind me." Riley groaned.

"You think Alex doesn't know his own mind?" Manuelo asked.

"Maybe he does now, but who knows what could happen?" Riley fed another piece of toast to Pepper. "Oh, well, at least it's Friday. I won't have to see her over the weekend."

Chloe finished her juice. "I hate to tell you, Riley, but it's only Thursday."

"It is? No!" Riley exclaimed.

"Check the newspaper," Chloe said, sliding it across the table.

Riley pulled the paper toward her. "Oh, no. It *is* Thursday!"

"It better be," Riley's mother said, glancing up from the counter. "I've got to get going on my new cruise wear line, and I'm still selecting the fabrics. I need every day I can get."

Manuelo turned toward the table and frowned. "Look at your backpack, Riley. It's torn at the bottom."

Riley glanced at the bulging backpack leaning against a table leg and spotted a small rip in the canvas. But who cared? She had more important things on her mind. "It's just a little tear," she said.

"And it's going to get a lot bigger," Manuelo told her. "Things will start to fall out, and then where will you be?"

"At the mall, getting a new one?" Chloe suggested.

"A waste of good money. There's no time to sew it now, but I have some blue tape that should match perfectly." Manuelo opened a drawer and took out a pair of scissors.

"I was so sure it was Friday," Riley said. "Now I have to watch Willow flirt with Alex for two more days instead of one."

"Look, why don't you clue Alex in?" Chloe suggested. "First tell Willow you found that notebook and you know what she's up to. Then tell Alex what's going on."

"Bad idea," Manuelo declared, lifting Riley's backpack onto the table. "Alex thinks Willow is a close friend, right?"

"So?" Chloe replied.

"Well, then such a plan would almost definitely backfire," Manuelo said, cutting a piece of dark blue tape from a roll. "Willow would deny the whole thing, and Riley would have no way to prove it. Then Alex would feel caught in the middle. It would put a cloud over his relationship with Riley. It could drive him straight into Willow's arms."

Riley groaned. "I definitely don't want that."

"So what's Riley supposed to do?" Chloe demanded.

"Nothing." Manuelo smoothed the tape over the rip in Riley's backpack.

"Come on, Manuelo, I have to do *something*," Riley said.

Manuelo shook his head. "Doing nothing will be hard, but it's often the best way. Trust me." He finished taping the backpack and returned to the counter. "There *is* one thing you might want to do," he added as he started putting together the girls' lunches.

"What?" Riley asked eagerly.

"Well…" Manuelo stuck bunches of grapes into the paper bags. "You might want to rethink your hair."

"What's the matter with it?" Riley asked. Both she and Chloe had blond hair, but Chloe's was longer and wavy. Riley usually wore hers down, but for the past few days she'd been pulling it back and clipping it behind her head. "I think this style makes me look older and sophisticated."

"Sorry, but you look like a fourteen-year-old who's *trying* to look older and sophisticated," Manuelo said.

Chloe studied Riley for a few seconds. "Manuelo might be right," she added.

"Of course I'm right." Manuelo glanced over his shoulder and grinned. "When am I not?"

[Riley: I guess you can tell that Manuelo isn't exactly modest.]

"Come on, Riley," Chloe said, taking her glass to the sink. "We have to go or we'll be late."

Macy glanced up again. "Wait," she said. "I've been meaning to tell you two—make sure you're free at seven Monday night. I've booked a photographer to come take a new family portrait. It's time we updated it."

Riley frowned. "Mom, is this because you and Dad have split and you want a picture without him?"

"Don't be ridiculous," Mrs. Carlson said. "Of course your father should be in the photograph. He's still part of the family. It's just that the only picture we have is ten years old."

Jake smiled and ran his fingers through his light

brown hair. "Well, then, I guess I should get a trim."

"Can Pepper be in the picture, too?" Riley asked. "She's part of the family now."

"If she'll hold still and not slobber, she can be in the picture," Macy agreed. "Think about what you want to wear," she added as Riley and Chloe headed for the door.

"I already know," Chloe said. "My favorite blue sweater. Except it's dirty. Manuelo—"

"Could you please take it to the dry cleaner?" Manuelo finished for her. "Yes."

"Great! Thanks!" Chloe opened the door. "Let's go, Riley."

As Riley started to follow, Manuelo called out to her. "Remember my advice, Riley."

"About what?"

"The Willow-Alex situation." Manuelo held a finger to his lips. "Don't say a word to either of them. Everything will work out the way it's supposed to."

Right, Riley thought. But would it be the way she wanted?

chapter
two

Later that morning in sewing class, Riley tried to concentrate on her latest project, a cover for a throw pillow. But she kept sneaking glances at Willow.

Larry Slotnick sat between Riley and Willow. He was tall and lanky, with brown hair and brown eyes. He lived next door to the Carlsons, and he'd had a crush on Riley since kindergarten.

"So, I finally got to you," Larry said the third time Riley glanced his way. "What was it? My incredibly strong jaw? My masculine chin?"

"Huh?" Riley asked.

"You keep staring at me," Larry said. Clearly, he didn't realize she was looking at Willow. He gave her a goofy grin. "I guess this means you'll go out with me now."

"Ohhh," Riley said. Larry was always asking her out. And Riley was always saying no. It was practically a game. He knew she liked him only as a friend. "Sorry,

Larry. It doesn't mean we're going out," she told him.

Larry shrugged. "Check out my muscles." He flexed a skinny arm. "Maybe you'll change your mind."

Riley rolled her eyes and went back to her pillow cover. A few minutes later Larry left his desk to talk to Ms. Spoke, the sewing teacher.

Riley took another quick glance at Willow. Tall and blond and incredibly pretty, Willow was making a blouse. Riley never would have tried a blouse. It was too hard, with sleeves and a collar and buttonholes. But Willow didn't seem to be having any trouble.

Of course, Willow didn't seem to have trouble with anything, Riley thought. She was smart and friendly. In her few weeks at West Malibu High she'd already made the swim team and organized a food drive for a local charity.

Willow suddenly rose from her sewing station and headed for the teacher's desk. Willow gave Riley a big smile before she walked past her. "Hey, Riley, I really like your sweater," she whispered. "You look so awesome in green."

"Thanks." Riley smiled back, but all of a sudden she felt worried. Did she really look good in green? Or did it make her skin seem sallow, and Willow wanted her to keep wearing it so she'd look terrible?

"See you later." Willow gave a little wave, then walked up to Ms. Spoke. A couple of seconds later she headed for the door, carrying a bathroom pass.

As soon as Willow was gone, Sierra Pomeroy, who

sat on Riley's left, stopped cutting fabric and leaned over.

Sierra's real name was Sarah, but the only people who ever called her that were her parents. Unfortunately, they were really conservative, unlike Sierra, and they made her wear boring clothes and play violin in the school orchestra.

Sierra liked the violin but didn't like the boring clothes. So she changed into cooler outfits as soon as she got to school. She also kept The Wave a secret from her parents, which Riley thought was a totally amazing feat, since Sierra was almost always practicing with the band.

"What did Willow say?" Sierra asked. She knew all about Willow's notebook.

"She *said* I look good in green," Riley replied skeptically. "Do I?"

Sierra shrugged. "You look okay."

"Only *okay*? I knew it—she wants me to look bad!" Riley sighed. "I wish I knew what to do about her. Manuelo says I shouldn't say anything to Alex. Maybe he's right. I mean, I can't prove Willow wants him back or anything."

"Probably not." Sierra grinned. "If she hadn't written his name all over her notebook with those pink hearts. That's proof, isn't it?"

"Yeah, but I don't have the book," Riley said. "Willow does."

Sierra glanced at Willow's sewing station, then at the

door. With another grin, she moved quickly to Willow's desk.

"What are you doing?" Riley demanded.

"Look." Sierra pointed to Willow's bag. It was unzipped, and poking out of the top was a dark red notebook. "Is that it?"

"I'm not sure. I guess…"

Sierra pulled out the notebook.

"Sierra, don't!" Riley whispered.

"Why not?" Sierra flipped it open. "There!" she exclaimed, jabbing her finger at the page of pink hearts. "There's the proof!"

"Yeah, but we can't just take it," Riley protested.

The bell rang, and the class started packing up to leave the room.

"Come on, Sierra," Riley said. "Put it back, okay?" Just as she reached for the notebook, a hand from behind her snatched it away.

"What do you think you're doing?" Willow demanded.

Riley gulped. She tried to think of some excuse, but she knew it was too late. She turned to Willow. "I…uh…"

Willow was clearly angry. "Why were you two snooping through my stuff?" she asked.

"We weren't snooping," Sierra said.

"Give me a break," Willow snapped. "I *saw* you."

Riley still hadn't thought of a good lie. I might as well tell the truth, she thought. At least Willow will know that I know what she's up to.

"I know what you're doing," Riley told her. "You're pretending to be nice to me so you can get closer to Alex. I know you want him back."

Here it comes, she thought. She's going to deny the whole thing.

Willow glanced at the open notebook in her hands. Then she looked at Riley. "So what if I do?" she said.

[Riley: Tell me, what do you say to something like that? I mean, what happened to being shy when you're the new girl in school? To knowing boundaries? To respecting the sisterhood of all girl-kind?]

Willow snapped the notebook closed and gave Riley a snide smile. "And guess what, Riley? I'm going to get him, too."

"Whoa," Sierra murmured.

Riley felt her face grow hot. She wasn't going to let Willow walk all over her. "Why don't you go ahead and try?" she said.

"I've already started," Willow told her. "And it'll be easy. I've known him way longer than you have. And we were crazy about each other. When I moved away, we sent E-mails to each other every day. He really, really missed me. I'll get him back. Wait and see."

[Riley: Oh, boy.]

• • •

13

There he is, Chloe thought. Travis Morgan. The guy she'd had a crush on since the beginning of freshman year. The guy she'd finally managed to go out with a few times.

He was tall and tan. And he was walking toward her down the hall.

"Travis, hey!" Chloe called.

He spotted her and waved. Immediately, Chloe's stomach felt as if a million butterflies were fluttering around in there. She kind of liked that feeling—the excitement, that is. The butterflies sort of made her want to hurl, but as long as she didn't hurl on Travis, she figured it was okay.

"What's up?" Travis said when he reached Chloe. He flashed her one of his amazing smiles.

[**Chloe**: He's-so-hot-he's-so-hot-he's-so-hot! Ahhhh! Okay. I feel better now. I just had to get that out.]

"Nothing much," Chloe replied, trying to keep her cool. "Just hanging out until class starts. I have business studies next."

"Oh," he said. "Want to get together at lunch?"

Chloe brightened. "Sure!" she said. Though they had lunch the same period, this was the first time Travis had actually asked her to eat with him. He usually hung out with his friends Kyle and Cameron.

"Cool." Travis smiled again. "See you later."

"Later," Chloe said, watching him saunter down the

hall. She made a mental note to put on some lip gloss before lunch.

"Chloe!" Riley said, coming toward her.

As soon as Chloe saw her sister, she could tell something had happened. And from the frown on Riley's face, she knew it wasn't good. "What's wrong?" she asked.

"Willow caught me looking at her notebook," Riley replied.

"Uh-oh. The one with Alex's name all over it?" Chloe asked. "What were you doing with it?"

"Sierra took it out, and—oh, never mind. It's a long story." Riley sighed. "But anyway, Willow just came right out and admitted that she wants Alex back. She said she'd get him, too!"

"Shh! Here she comes," Chloe whispered. "Incredible—she's smiling at us!"

"Hi, you guys," Willow said as she approached them. "Hey, does anybody know what we're doing in class today?"

Riley shook her head.

Chloe shrugged. "More stuff about the economy, I guess."

Willow grinned. "Are you as bored with it as I am?"

Chloe nodded. How could Willow act so friendly? she wondered.

"I just hope I don't fall asleep," Willow said with a laugh. "Well, see you guys inside!"

After Willow left, Riley rolled her eyes. "Who does she think she's fooling?"

[<u>Chloe</u>: **I didn't want to say this to Riley, but Willow is a great actress. I mean, if I weren't Riley's sister, I would totally think Willow was a nice person. I'd probably even be friends with her! But that's just between you and me.**]

"Okay, this is war," Chloe declared. "You have to tell Alex about Willow now."

"But Willow will deny it," Riley said. "She'll say I made it up because I'm jealous of her friendship with Alex. She'll say *something* that'll make me look bad, and Alex won't know which one of us to believe. It'll be a mess—just like Manuelo said it would!"

Chloe shook her head. "It's already a mess."

"I know." Riley groaned. "But I don't want to make it worse. I'll stick with Manuelo's advice and keep my mouth shut. For now, anyway."

The bell rang, and Riley groaned again. "I guess we have to go in."

As Chloe and Riley turned toward the door, Larry came rushing up to them. "Hi, Chloe. Hi, Riley!" he exclaimed, smiling happily. "Hey, Riley, can I look at your notes for a minute, just in case Miss Westmore calls on me?"

"Sure." Riley trudged through the door with Larry on her heels.

As Chloe followed them inside, the first person she noticed was Willow, naturally. She was laughing and chatting with the girl sitting behind her.

Chloe took her seat and tried to pay attention as Miss Westmore discussed the economy and the job market. But her mind kept drifting. First to Riley and Alex and then to Travis.

Tall, with sandy-brown hair and mesmerizing green eyes, Travis was one of the coolest guys in school. And Chloe practically melted every time he looked at her. She was really glad he didn't have a Willow in his past. The only thing Chloe had to compete with was his dirt bike. And his dirt-bike buddies.

Still, at least it's not a girl, she thought, smiling to herself. She glanced across the room at Riley. Her sister seemed to be listening, but Chloe knew better. Riley's mind was on Alex.

Chloe turned her thoughts back to Travis. I can't wait to have lunch with him, she decided happily. This is a big step. After all, don't *boyfriends* usually have lunch with their *girlfriends*?

Okay, so they weren't "official" yet. Who cared? In her opinion, four, which was the number of dates they'd had so far, was enough for her to unofficially call him her official boyfriend.

Hmm, I wonder if he feels the same, Chloe thought.

"All right, class, time is almost up," Miss Westmore said, breaking into Chloe's thoughts. "Before you go, remember your assignment for Career Week. It starts next Monday."

Assignment? Chloe quickly flipped through her notebook. There it was—Career Week. Everyone was supposed to invite someone to talk to the class about what he or she did for a living.

Chloe groaned to herself. She'd forgotten all about it. And Miss Westmore always went alphabetically, which meant Chloe and Riley would be up on Monday.

Chloe scanned her notes about the assignment again.

Someone w/intrstng. job or who admire. Could be neighbor, parent, etc.

Parent? Chloe smiled. Maybe she'd found the answer.

The bell rang, and everyone stampeded out. Everyone except Willow, Chloe noticed, who stayed behind to talk to Miss Westmore. Teacher's pet, Chloe thought.

"Come on, let's go before Willow comes out," Riley said as she joined Chloe in the hall. "I couldn't stand to have her act nice to me again."

"Forget about Willow for a second," Chloe said. "What about the Career Week assignment? Do you know who you're inviting?"

Riley shook her head. "I kept forgetting to remind myself about it."

"Me, too," Chloe admitted. "But I just got a great

idea—we'll do it together. Mom and Dad can be our speakers!"

Riley frowned. "Mom's okay, but Dad doesn't really have a job anymore, remember? Reading the latest yoga book isn't exactly the kind of career Miss Westmore is thinking of."

"Oh. Right." Chloe sighed. "I thought I had the perfect solution. I guess we'll each have to ask somebody different."

"Yeah," Riley agreed.

"No, wait," Chloe said. "We can't do that. If one of us asks Mom, it'll hurt Dad's feelings. But if we invite other people, we'll hurt both their feelings."

"Chloe, we have to invite somebody," Riley argued.

Chloe nodded. "Okay, here's what we do—we each ask someone, but we don't tell Mom or Dad about it."

"You mean we should keep it a secret?" Riley asked.

"Yeah, but it's for a good cause," Chloe insisted. "We're not really trying to fool anyone. We just don't want to hurt Mom's and Dad's feelings, right?"

"I guess so," Riley said doubtfully.

"Good." Chloe grinned. "Don't worry, Riley, it'll just be a tiny little secret."

Giving Riley a wave, Chloe hurried down the hall. She still had to find someone for Career Week, but she'd worry about that later. Right now it was time for lunch—and for Travis.

chapter
three

A few minutes later, Chloe was sitting in the cafeteria with her friend Amanda Gray. Amanda ate lasagna while Chloe sipped apple juice and watched the door for Travis.

"Aren't you going to eat?" Amanda asked. She pointed to Chloe's untouched Swiss-cheese sandwich.

"Sure." Chloe picked up half the sandwich, then put it down. "I wish Travis would hurry up!" she said.

"Why don't you go find him?" Amanda suggested.

[Chloe: Amanda _would_ say something like that. She just doesn't realize how uncool it would look to go searching for Travis. Of course, Amanda doesn't care about being cool. Which is actually kind of cool itself, when you think about it.]

Chloe picked up her sandwich again and took a bite. "He'll be here. After all, it was his idea for us to eat together. He probably had to go to his locker. Or maybe his teacher kept the class late or something."

Tucking a strand of light brown hair behind her ear, Amanda glanced toward the door. "Or maybe he's in detention," she suggested.

"Very funny." When Chloe first met him, Travis was one of the guys who was always getting into trouble. Nothing major, just enough to get plenty of detention. "He's reformed."

But not *that* reformed, Chloe thought. He wasn't late because he was doing an extra-credit project—she was sure of that. So why was he late?

Chloe ate a bit more of sandwich, keeping one eye on the door. This wasn't the first time Travis was late. Once, his best friend needed help starting his dirt bike, so Travis was way late meeting her at her locker. Another time, he said he'd call her at eight but didn't call until after nine because he was out and he didn't have a cell phone.

And now he was late for lunch—after *he'd* asked *her* to eat with him. Chloe started to feel a little panicky. Had Travis totally forgotten her?

Alex wouldn't forget Riley, Chloe thought. He always put Riley first. But maybe that was different. They were officially boyfriend and girlfriend. She and Travis weren't.

"There he is," Amanda announced.

Chloe's gaze snapped to the door. There he was, all right.

Brown-haired, green-eyed, and totally cute, he waved and began making his way toward Chloe's table.

Chloe waved and smiled. One look at Travis and the fluttery feeling was back. He hadn't forgotten!

"Hi." Smiling at Chloe and Amanda, Travis leaned against the edge of the table and eyed the remaining half of Chloe's sandwich. "Mind if I have a bite of that? I'm starving. Sorry I'm late, by the way."

"That's okay." Chloe handed him the sandwich. "What happened?" she asked as he took a big bite. "I mean, you asked me to meet you at lunch."

Travis nodded. "I know. It's just that I ran into Kyle and Cameron and we started talking," he explained.

Oh, great, Chloe thought, feeling hurt and angry. His dirt-bike buddies are more important than I am!

"I finally noticed the time and split," Travis went on. "Told the guys I had to meet my girlfriend." He grinned at Chloe and polished off the sandwich.

[Chloe: Did you hear that? He called me his girl-friend! And just last period I was thinking about the very same thing. This is so incredible!]

Chloe's anger totally vanished, and she smiled back. She started to suggest they eat lunch together the next day, when the bell rang.

Travis pushed away from the table. "I'd better hurry. I have to hike all the way to the other side of the building. Thanks for lunch," he added. "See you later."

"Did you hear what he said?" Chloe exclaimed as Travis hurried off. "He called me his girlfriend! It's official now. Is that great, or what?"

"It's great," Amanda agreed, picking up her tray. "Does 'official' mean he won't be late all the time anymore?"

"Well…he's not a clock watcher, so I'm not sure," Chloe said. She wadded up her empty lunch bag. "But it means he's really serious about me, so who cares if he's a little late once in a while?"

I can live with late, Chloe thought. As long as I have Travis, I can live with anything!

"Are you looking for somebody?" Alex asked Riley that afternoon as they walked down the hall together. "You keep glancing over your shoulder."

"No," Riley said. But it wasn't true. Of course she was looking for someone—Willow, to be exact. Somehow, Willow always managed to show up when Riley and Alex were together. "I was just…I don't know. Looking around, that's all."

Alex reached out and took her hand. "Too bad I have history class now," he said. "I'd rather go to the library with you."

"Me, too," Riley agreed. She stopped glancing around and paid total attention to Alex, which was much more fun. She liked the way he looked, naturally. But she liked who he was just as much. Maybe even more. He was kind of shy and quiet, but he had lots of intense feelings that came out in the songs he wrote. "Hey, you want to get a Coke after school?"

"I can't. The band is practicing." Alex squeezed her hand. "We're trying to work the kinks out of a new arrangement."

Oh, well, Riley thought. "What about tonight?" she asked. "You could come over after dinner."

"Maybe," Alex said. "I have a major test in Spanish tomorrow, but I'll try." He squeezed her hand again.

Riley squeezed back, smiling. But her smile faded as Willow rounded the corner and hurried toward them.

"Hi, you two!" Willow exclaimed happily. "Alex, I was hoping I'd run into you."

[Riley: Hoping? Plotting is more like it.]

Riley forced a smile. "Hi, Willow."

"What's up?" Alex asked.

"I just wanted to double-check about what time I should come to your house tonight," Willow told him.

Riley glanced at Willow. *She's* going to Alex's house? How come?

"About seven," Alex said to Willow. "Maybe a little after. Mom will definitely be home by then."

"What's this about?" Riley asked, trying to sound casual.

Willow turned to Riley. A sneaky little gleam appeared in her eyes. "Alex's mom is on the town council," she explained. "And since I'm interested in politics, I'm going to ask her to be my Career Week speaker. I haven't seen her since I moved back. It'll be so much fun to talk to her again!"

[Riley: See that sparkle in her eye? Willow's letting me know that she'll be at Alex's house tonight—and I won't. Sure, she'll be talking to his mother, but you can bet she'll figure out a way to spend some time with Alex, too—probably alone. She's even sneakier than I thought she was. I have to do something! But what?]

chapter
four

"**I** can't stand it!" Riley declared, staring at the clock in the kitchen that evening. She was supposed to be studying biology, but she couldn't concentrate. "Willow is at Alex's house right now!"

Manuelo looked up from the counter where he was checking out Riley's broken hair dryer. "You told me she was interviewing his mother. And that Alex has to study for a test."

"Oh, Manuelo, that doesn't matter." Riley groaned. "Willow takes Spanish, too. As soon as she finishes talking to his mom, she'll probably say, 'Hey, Alex, as long as I'm here, let's study together!' And Alex will think it's a great idea because he doesn't have a clue what she's up to."

"Ah—look at this." Manuelo held up the hair dryer's cord. "The cord is frayed. Fortunately, I am handy enough to fix the problem."

"Good. Too bad you can't fix my problem with Willow," Riley said.

"I already gave you advice on that," he replied.

"I know, and I haven't said anything to Alex," Riley told him. "But Willow's being so sneaky, Manuelo! Are you sure I should keep quiet about this?"

"Positive. If Alex truly cares for you, Willow won't get anywhere with him." Manuelo picked up the dryer. "Now. I'm taking this into the garage to put a new cord on it. Then I have to get some clothes together for the dry cleaner. Do you want me to take your yellow silk top so you can wear it for the family portrait on Monday?"

"That would be great. I almost forgot about the picture," Riley said. "Thanks, Manuelo."

"At your service." Manuelo bowed from the waist, then picked up the hair dryer and left the kitchen.

Riley turned back to her biology notes. She spent about ten seconds studying a diagram of a worm, but it was impossible not to think of Willow.

Riley had major doubts about keeping quiet. She really, really wanted Alex to know what was going on, but she didn't have a good way to tell him. Maybe Sierra could help. Maybe she could talk to him.

[Riley: Okay, so maybe it's the chicken's way out. But it could work, couldn't it? Here's how I see it:

Sierra: Alex, Willow wants to get back together with you.

Alex: No way. We're just good friends.

Sierra: That's what you think. She wrote your name in pink hearts all over her notebook. (She cleverly doesn't mention me.)

Later, Alex would most definitely confront Willow:

Willow (after Alex tells her what Sierra said): Oh, Alex, it's true, but I wanted to keep it to myself! (She starts to cry.) If only Sierra and Riley hadn't snooped through my bag!

Alex (shocked): Riley went through your stuff?

Willow (nods and sniffs): I'm sorry, Alex.

Alex (looks sympathetic—also flattered): Don't be sorry. It's not your fault. (He puts his arms around her as the curtain falls.)]

Riley shook her head. Forget it. Getting Sierra to talk to Alex was definitely a bad plan.

As Riley tried to study her science notes again, Chloe opened the kitchen door, leading Pepper in on a leash.

"I walked all the way over to the trailer park for nothing," Chloe announced, unclipping the dog's leash. Travis's family lived in the same trailer park as their dad did—Vista del Mar. "Travis wasn't home. Not that he said he would be, but—" A noise outside the kitchen door interrupted her. "Maybe that's him!" she said.

Or Alex, Riley thought hopefully. Maybe he's not spending any time with Willow after all.

Chloe opened the door.

Larry stood in the doorway. Riley was a little surprised. Not because it was Larry—he came over all the time. But he didn't always arrive dressed in a full-body lobster costume, complete with claws and bobbing antennae.

"Hi, guys," he said, waving a claw at them.

Chloe and Riley burst out laughing. Pepper growled.

"How do I look?" Larry asked.

"Like you need a squeeze of lemon," Chloe told him.

Riley couldn't stop laughing. Larry was wrapped in a puffy red shell from the top of his head to the middle of his thighs. He wore red tights on his legs and red rubber flippers on his feet. "Uh, Larry? I think Halloween's over," she said.

"Yeah, so you're probably wondering why I'm dressed like a lobster."

"Well…" Actually, Riley wasn't that surprised anymore. This was goofy Larry, after all.

"I got a job at Neptune's Net," Larry announced proudly. "I'm the Welcome Lobster. I show people to their tables and give them their menus." He did a little dance that made his lobster antennae bob around.

Riley couldn't help laughing again.

"Go ahead, make fun," Larry said. "Greeting people at a restaurant happens to be an important job. Public relations, you know."

Riley bit her lip and choked back another laugh. "Sorry, Larry. It's cool that you have a job."

29

"It is," he agreed. "And listen, if you don't have any-body to be your Career Week speaker yet, well...I'm here for you, Riley."

"Thanks, Larry. I'll remember that," Riley said, trying to sound grateful.

"Just let me know, because if you don't need me, I might be my own speaker!" Waving a claw, Larry turned to leave. One of his flippers caught on the doorframe. He finally pulled it loose and waddled away.

As Chloe shut the door, Riley put her head in her hands. "Career Day!" She groaned. "I still haven't thought of anyone yet. Have you?"

Chloe shook her head.

"We don't have much time," Riley reminded her. "Only three days!"

"I know. I keep telling myself I'll find somebody," Chloe said. "But first I'm going to go call Travis. Maybe he's home by now." Chloe picked up the cordless phone and left the kitchen.

Riley sat at the table and tried to think of someone to bring to Career Week. After all, it was an important assignment. But she kept thinking about Willow and Alex instead. Finally she gave up on Career Week, for the moment, at least. After all, if she didn't have anyone by Sunday night, there was always Larry the Lobster.

As Chloe headed for the kitchen on Friday morning, the doorbell rang. She turned and hurried through the living room toward the front door to answer it.

It's not Travis, she told herself. Why do you even think it is? He wasn't home when you stopped by or called last night, and you didn't leave a message. Besides, he always sleeps as late as possible.

Still, Chloe couldn't help feeling hopeful. Now that she was his official girlfriend, Travis just might decide to drop by and surprise her. She took a quick look in the hall mirror, fluffed her hair, and pulled open the door. "Oh. Tedi."

"Good morning to you, too," Tedi said, peering at Chloe over her sunglasses.

Tedi was Macy Carlson's friend. She was also a model. A beautiful model, with dark hair, perfect skin, and a great body.

"Sorry," Chloe said. "Come on in."

Tedi swept inside. She wore a gorgeous backless gown and a glittering choker around her neck.

"Cool outfit," Chloe said. "Where are you going?"

"Going? I'm just coming back. I was at a boutique opening in Beverly Hills. It turned into an all-nighter," Tedi explained. "Where's your mom? She wanted to talk to me about her new cruise-wear line, and I decided to drop by on my way home."

"Mom's still in the shower. Want to come into the kitchen and have some coffee?" Chloe asked.

"Thanks, but I can't stay," Tedi said. "I have to go grab a couple hours of sleep, and then I have three jobs this afternoon and another party tonight. A supermodel's life is not easy! Just tell your mom I'll call, and—"

"Teddy, you're a supermodel!" Chloe suddenly cried.

"That's me," Tedi agreed.

"Wait." Chloe listened for a second. The shower was still going. "Listen, Tedi," she whispered, "could we talk about something? But it's got to be a secret. You can never, ever tell Mom."

Tedi lowered her sunglasses. "Ooh, is this about a boy?"

"No. Career Week." Chloe quickly explained the situation. "So will you be my speaker?" she whispered. "You'd be totally perfect."

Tedi whipped a Palm Pilot out of her beaded evening bag and brought up her calendar. "Monday morning? You're in luck. I have a little free time."

"Great! Thanks, Tedi," Chloe said. "Just remember, don't say anything to Mom."

"Not a word," Tedi promised. "See you Monday."

Chloe closed the door and sighed with relief. At least that's out of the way, she thought. And Tedi would be a major hit in class. Now Chloe could concentrate on more important things—like being Travis's girlfriend.

chapter five

Riley started to feel slightly anxious in business studies class as the other kids announced their Career Week speakers.

Willow was bringing Alex's mom, of course. Zach Block had invited his uncle, who designed computer games. Lindsay Fullham's neighbor was a TV producer.

And this morning, when Larry offered to be Riley's speaker again, she turned him down. So Larry had definitely decided to come on his own behalf as the Welcome Lobster.

And Riley's own sister had snagged the best of all— an actual fashion model! Riley could have kicked herself for not thinking of Tedi.

Am I the only one who hasn't invited anybody yet? Riley wondered. She slouched down in her chair, hoping Miss Westmore wouldn't call on her.

It didn't work. It never worked.

"Let's see," Miss Westmore said, her small brown eyes roaming over the class. "Ah—Riley. What about you? Who are you bringing for Career Week?"

"I...well, I have a couple of people in mind, and I'm just trying to decide," Riley replied. Her thoughts raced, trying to come up with some fake possibilities. Fortunately, Chloe came to her rescue by "accidentally" knocking a book off her desk. It landed with a loud slap, and everyone jumped. Then the bell rang, and Riley was saved.

"Thanks for the interruption," Riley said as she and Chloe left the classroom.

"No problem," Chloe told her. "I'll catch you later, okay? I'm meeting you-know-who by his locker." She sped off.

"Hi, Riley," someone said.

Riley scowled at the sound of the voice. It was Willow's. She put on a blank face and turned around.

"I thought you'd like to know that I had a great time with Alex last night," Willow said. The nasty gleam was back in her eyes.

"Gee, thanks for telling me," Riley said. "But who cares? Didn't you go over to talk to his mother?"

"I did." Willow grinned. "But I spent plenty of time with Alex, too. Alone."

Riley gritted her teeth. She was dying to know what happened, but no way would she ask. That was exactly what Willow wanted.

"And guess what else?" Willow said.

Riley sighed. "Willow, I really don't care," she said, even though she did. She turned to walk away.

"Well, I'll tell you anyway," Willow said. "Alex's mom had some other things to do last night, and we couldn't finish. So I'm going back tomorrow afternoon. And Mrs. Zimmer said something about my staying for dinner. Isn't that nice?"

Oh, just great, Riley thought. Her jaw ached from clenching her teeth, but she had to keep quiet. She couldn't let Willow know she was getting to her!

Willow laughed softly. "I told you it would be easy, didn't I? Pretty soon Alex and I will get closer. He'll start to realize that he likes me way more than he'll ever like you. Then we'll be back together. And sooner than you think."

Willow walked away, still laughing.

Riley felt like screaming. Actually, she felt like running after Willow and screaming at *her*. Instead, she hurried through the halls to the music room. Alex played in the school jazz band and would just be getting out of practice. She hadn't seen him today and she missed him. Plus she wondered if anything had changed. She didn't want to believe what Willow said, but Alex *was* alone with her last night....

Of course, Riley couldn't come right out and ask if Willow put the moves on him or anything. But she could check for signs. Being in too much of a hurry to talk wouldn't be good. Not holding her hand would be bad.

Looking guilty would be a disaster. Stressed about the awful possibilities, Riley didn't even see Alex until she almost bumped into him.

"Whoa!" Alex laughed. "What's the rush?"

"I didn't want to miss you," Riley replied.

"I would have waited," he told her. He nudged Riley's shoulder, and they began walking together.

[**Riley:** He said he would have waited. That's good. But he's not holding my hand. Why isn't he holding my hand?]

"Is something wrong?" Alex asked.

"Huh? No...Why?"

He shrugged. "You look worried or something."

"Oh." Riley thought fast. "Right. I am. I still don't have anybody for Career Week and Miss Westmore's not exactly an easy grader."

[**Riley:** That's not a total lie. I am worried about finding a speaker. I'm just more worried about Willow.]

"You'll find somebody," Alex assured her. "I'll try to think of someone for you, too." He took Riley's hand.

[**Riley:** Yes! An excellent sign!]

Riley took a deep breath and began to relax. As far as she could tell, nothing had changed between her and Alex. But that didn't mean it couldn't. After all, Riley knew that Willow wouldn't give up without a fight.

"Hey, there's Willow," Alex said, interrupting Riley's thoughts.

Riley groaned to herself.

Keeping hold of Riley's hand, Alex pulled her toward Willow, who was waving at them from down the hallway.

"Hi, Riley." Willow gave Riley a bright, friendly smile.

Riley made herself smile back. "Hi, Willow."

"I like that clip you're using to hold your hair back," Willow said. "I just love silver."

"It's plastic," Riley replied. She couldn't keep the coolness out of her voice, and Alex gave her a funny look.

Watch it, Riley told herself. He thinks Willow's great, remember?

"Well, it's a pretty hair clip, anyway," Willow said. Turning up the wattage on her smile, she looked at Alex. "I had so much fun last night!"

Alex laughed. "Me, too."

[Riley: Oh, no! Fun with Willow? That's a bad sign. Really bad.]

"We watched a game show in Spanish on cable," Alex explained to Riley. "I bombed, but Willow did really well."

"It's such an awesome way to study the language,"

Willow said. Her eyes sparkled as she looked at Riley.

"Cool," Riley said, smiling at her.

[Riley: I can't stand this! I am going to explode!]

Willow turned back to Alex. "I'm glad I ran into you. I wanted to check with you about the time tomorrow," Willow went on. "My dad's dropping me off at two, but if your mom's not there yet, you'll let me in, right?"

"Right. I'll be there," Alex replied.

"I need to meet with his mom again," Willow added, smiling at Riley.

"You told me that four minutes ago," Riley snapped. "You don't have to remind me." She knew she sounded angry, and she almost didn't care. Except for one thing—Alex was staring at her as if she'd just sprouted horns.

Willow looked confused. Then she laughed a little. "That's right. I forgot. Riley and I were talking after business studies," she added to Alex. "Well, I'd better get going. See you tomorrow, Alex. Bye, Riley."

"Bye." Riley took a deep breath and forced herself to look at Alex.

He was frowning. "What was that all about?"

"What do you mean?" Riley said.

"The way you acted toward Willow," he said. "You weren't exactly friendly. I mean, you guys don't have to be best friends or anything, but can't you at least give her a break? She really likes you. Last night she even mentioned how smart you are and what a great sense of humor you have." He paused as if he were trying to find the right words. "She's a good friend of mine, Riley. Just try to be a little nicer to her, okay?"

How could you be so clueless, Alex, Riley wondered.

Riley wanted to defend herself. She wanted to tell him what Willow was *really* up to. But she couldn't—not after Willow had said all those nice things about her.

Besides, Willow probably wanted Riley and Alex to fight over her. And Riley wasn't about to do that.

"I'm sorry," Riley told him. "I'm just so stressed about that Career Week thing. I really didn't mean to sound so sarcastic to Willow."

"Maybe you should explain it to Willow. I could tell she was kind of hurt." Alex squeezed Riley's hand. "Don't worry. She'll understand."

[Riley: Can you believe this? He actually thinks Willow is a sweet, understanding person! Somebody really needs to clue him in. I wish it could be me.]

Later that day Chloe waited eagerly in front of Travis's locker after school. When she ran into him earlier, he suggested that they meet and go get pizza. Naturally, she said yes. Now she couldn't wait to see him again.

"Hi, Chloe," a girl named Joelle Myers said as she walked by. Chloe didn't know her very well. "Did you forget your combination?"

"Huh? Oh, no," Chloe replied. "This isn't my locker. It's my boyfriend's. I'm waiting for him."

She smiled. Her *boyfriend's*. That was the first time she ever said that to anybody. She liked the sound of it!

And she was looking forward to having a really close relationship with Travis. She already knew him a little, but she didn't *really* know him. Now that he was her boyfriend they'd have lots of in-depth conversations. They'd be able to share their hopes, their dreams...their everything!

Chloe glanced down the hall. There was Travis, rounding the corner. Her stomach fluttered. Her heart thumped.

"Hi," Travis said, smiling at her.

Chloe's stomach fluttered again. Her heart thumped harder. "Ready for pizza?" she asked. "I'm starving."

"Yeah, me, too," Travis said. "But let's go out to the parking lot for a minute first. Kyle's still having trouble with his bike, and I told him I'd take a look at it."

"Oh. Okay," Chloe said. The heart-thumping slowed a bit.

"It won't take long." Travis gave her a sexy grin as he opened his locker.

Chloe's heart sped up again. So what if she had to wait a little while for him to look at his friend's bike? They'd be together, wouldn't they? That was the important thing.

● ● ●

On Saturday, Riley sat on her bed watching Chloe brush her hair. "Where are you going?" she asked.

"I'm taking Pepper for a walk. We're going to stop by and see Dad. And Travis, if he's home."

"Didn't you ask him if he'd be there?"

"Yes, but he said he wasn't sure," Chloe replied. "I hope he's there. And I hope Kyle's *not*. I had to wait a whole hour while he and Travis fiddled with that bike yesterday."

Riley grinned. "But it was worth the wait, right?"

"Sure, but I just wish..." Chloe hesitated.

"What?" Riley asked.

"Well, how long did it take before you and Alex were really close?" she asked.

Riley thought about it. "I don't know. I guess it all kind of happened pretty fast," she said. "It was as if I knew him all my life the very day we met."

"Oh," Chloe said. She gave her hair one last brush-stroke and hurried toward the door. "Gotta go."

"Say hi to your *boyfriend* for me," Riley said.

Chloe laughed and left the room.

Sighing, Riley settled back on her bed and picked up her list of possible Career Week people. There were only three. Two fashion magazine editors and her parents' investment banker. She sneaked the phone numbers from her mother's address book. And she'd planned to swear whoever said yes to total secrecy.

But it didn't matter now. It was Saturday, and nobody was home. The situation was entering the emergency stage. Riley had to find somebody to come to class by Monday.

She glanced at the clock. Almost two. Oh, no—two! Willow would be on her way to Alex's house.

Maybe I should call him, she thought. She picked up the phone from the nightstand and dialed.

It rang once, twice…

"Hello?" Alex answered.

"Hey…Alex!" Riley said a little too enthusiastically.

"Riley, what's up?" he asked.

Okay, Riley thought. He sounds glad to hear from me. The only problem was, she couldn't think of anything to say.

"Riley? Are you still there?" he asked.

"Yeah," Riley said.

"Hi, Riley!" Willow called from the background.

Riley bit her lip. Willow was already there.

"Willow says hi," Alex said. He started laughing.

"What's so funny?" Riley asked.

Alex laughed harder. "Willow…cut…it…out! You know I'm ticklish!"

Willow giggled in the background. "Make me!" she cried.

Riley bit her lip harder. She didn't want to jump to conclusions. She didn't want to say anything that she'd regret later. So she just said, "Call me later, okay?" Then she hung up.

Good, Riley thought. At least Willow will think I

trust Alex. But do I? What are they doing over there? she wondered.

No, no, no! Don't think about that, Riley ordered herself. She slid off the bed and paced a little, trying to think of other people for Career Week, but she drew a blank.

After pacing another minute, Riley decided a Coke would help wake up her brain. She stuffed the list into her backpack so her mom wouldn't spot it and ask questions. Mom was out getting her hair cut at the moment, but Riley wasn't taking any chances.

She was popping the top on her Coke when Manuelo came into the kitchen carrying two grocery bags and a six-pack of soda. She took a sip of her drink and sighed loudly.

"Ah, I see I'm just in time," Manuelo said. Setting the groceries on the table, he unpacked a jar of chocolate sauce. "What's wrong? Is it the Willow situation?"

"No. Well, yes, but there's something else, too," Riley told him. She wanted to keep her mind off Willow. "Manuelo, can you keep a secret?"

He raised an eyebrow. "Riley, I have worked in this house for fourteen years. I have secrets buried inside me. For instance..." He glanced around, then lowered his voice. "Do you know who walks off with the chocolate sauce and takes it back to his trailer?"

"Hmm, that's a tough one," Riley said. "Could it be Dad?"

Manuelo put a finger to his lips. "I can't tell you. It's a secret."

"Okay, here's the problem," Riley said. "Monday starts Career Week in our business studies class. We're supposed to invite people to come talk about their jobs, but I don't have anybody yet. Chloe and I decided we couldn't ask Mom without asking Dad. And we can't ask Dad because he doesn't have a job. So we didn't ask either one of them."

"And you've kept them in the dark to spare their feelings," Manuelo said. "Very thoughtful."

"Yeah, except I don't have anybody to bring to class!" Riley exclaimed. "And Chloe went off and got Tedi."

"Ooh, a supermodel."

Riley nodded. "I'm really getting desperate. And it's even too late to ask the Welcome Lobster!"

"The what?" Manuelo asked.

Riley explained about Larry's job at Neptune's Net and how he'd offered to be her speaker. "I figured I could find somebody else, but I can't. And I need someone by Monday morning."

"Well, it shouldn't be that hard," Manuelo told her, pulling a bunch of carrots out of one of the grocery bags.

"How can you say that?" Riley asked. "Manuelo, I need somebody professional. Somebody dynamic. Somebody outstanding in his field."

Manuelo straightened his shoulders and proudly lifted his chin. "And I will be there!"

"You will?" Riley asked.

"Yes, and don't worry," Manuelo whispered. "This will be our little secret."

"This is great, Manuelo. Thanks!" Riley said. She *was* grateful, but she couldn't help feeling a little worried. What was Manuelo going to talk about—cooking and vacuuming? Everybody would be totally bored. She might even get a lousy grade.

But at least the Career Week problem was solved, she thought. Now if only she could solve the Willow problem!

chapter
six

On Monday morning Riley listened nervously as Chloe introduced Tedi to the class. Manuelo was the next speaker, and Riley had the feeling that a supermodel would be a hard act to follow.

"So here she is," Chloe announced proudly. "Someone who will give us an in-depth look at the world of fashion modeling—Tedi!"

Chloe pushed a button on her portable CD player, and Tedi entered the room to a pounding rock beat. Everyone clapped.

Wearing black leather pants, a crimson blouse, and six-inch heels, Tedi strode forward as if she were on a runway. At the front of the class, she turned and struck a pose. She took off the jacket, slung it over one shoulder, and posed again.

"That's what a fashion model does," Tedi announced as Chloe turned off the music.

Laura Tomson raised her hand. "How did you get to be a model?"

"Great cheekbones," Tedi replied. "And I knew an agent."

"How much money do you make?" Robert Shaw asked.

Tedi shifted to another pose. "Piles of it."

Sebastian Lee waved a hand in the air. "Have you ever done the *Sports Illustrated* swimsuit edition?" he asked with a grin.

Tedi grinned back. "Check out the millennium issue."

Someone else started to ask a question, but Tedi's pager beeped. She took it from her jacket pocket, read the message, and slipped her jacket back on. "Sorry, Chloe, it's a last-minute booking, and I've got to go. It's been fun, kids."

Waving to the class, Tedi swept out of the room.

"Well, that was certainly...brief," Miss Westmore said.

"Yeah, but at least it wasn't boring," Sebastian said.

"All right, who's next?" Miss Westmore asked.

"I am." Riley stood up and glanced to the back of the room where Manuelo was waiting. She hoped *he* wasn't boring, but it was too late to do anything about it now.

Riley walked to the front of the class. "My guest is Manuelo Del Valle," she announced. "He's been with my family for years, and he's going to talk about the... um...stuff he does."

Everyone clapped again, but Riley could tell the

kids were just being polite. As Manuelo came forward, rolling a cart in front of him, Sebastian yawned and pulled out a car magazine.

"Thank you, Riley, for that inspired introduction," he murmured. "Don't sit down yet. I'll need an assistant."

An assistant? What was he planning to do? Riley wondered.

Manuelo turned to the class. "Good morning. Indeed, my name is Manuelo. I am a professional domestic. Any questions?"

Silence.

Riley's heart sank. Manuelo was bombing already. She glanced at Miss Westmore, who was frowning.

I'm going to flunk this assignment, Riley thought.

Suddenly, Manuelo reached over and plucked the auto magazine from Sebastian's hands. "Any questions?" he repeated.

Sebastian yawned. "So, like, what do you do? House-cleaning and ironing and junk?"

"Yes, I do those things. And much, much more," Manuelo said. "Riley?"

Riley jumped, startled.

Manuelo snapped his fingers. "The jeans, please!"

Riley peered into the top part of the cart and saw a pair of ripped, faded jeans. "These?" she asked, holding them up.

Manuelo nodded. "We all have jeans like these at home," he told the class. "They're tattered. They're worn.

They're so bad, even a punk rocker wouldn't wear them. So what do you do with them?"

"Toss 'em," Sebastian muttered.

"Ah. That's why I'm a professional and you're not," Manuelo told him. "Let me show you what Manuelo does. Riley, the needle and thread."

Riley reached into the cart again and held up a spool of blue thread with a needle stuck into it.

"These, and a little imagination, are all you need," Manuelo said. "And look what you get! Riley?"

Riley pulled something from the cart and held it up. "Hey, it's a denim purse."

"Yes. Old jeans become a new purse." Taking the purse from Riley, Manuelo tossed it to Amanda in the back of the class.

"Thanks," Amanda told him. "This is really nice."

"And there's more!" Manuelo declared.

Getting into the spirit of it, Riley pulled out a denim wallet, a beaded belt, and a baseball cap. Manuelo tossed the wallet and the belt to two other kids, then put the baseball cap on Sebastian's head.

Sebastian took it off, checked it out, and put it back on. "Cool!" he said, not looking bored anymore.

"Manuelo, thank you!" Riley cried as the class laughed and applauded. "That was great!"

"Was?" Manuelo grinned. "Riley, I am just getting started."

From the cart, Manuelo brought out a hotplate, a

frying pan, and a bunch of food containers. While the pan heated, he put on a white jacket and a tall white chef's hat. With Riley handing him the ingredients, he quickly whipped up a batch of "Nachos Del Valle."

"And now, while my assistant serves you, it's time for a makeover!" Manuelo announced. "Miss Westmore, are you ready?"

Miss Westmore blushed. The class laughed and clapped as Manuelo led her to her desk chair and spun it around so its back was to the room.

While Riley passed out paper plates and served up the food, Manuelo brought out eye shadow, mascara, blush, and lipstick and began giving the teacher a makeover.

After a few minutes, Manuelo spun the chair around. "*Voilà!*" he announced. "A new Miss Westmore!"

"Whoa!" Larry exclaimed. "Miss Westmore, is that really you?"

Riley could hardly believe it. Miss Westmore's eyes seemed huge, and her face glowed. She actually looked pretty.

"Manuelo, you're amazing!" Miss Westmore exclaimed, gazing into the mirror he handed her.

"I truly am," he agreed. He turned to the class and bowed with a flourish. "This concludes my Career Week presentation!"

The kids in the class erupted into cheers and rose to their feet in a standing ovation.

Manuelo bowed again, then began putting his materials back in the cart.

"Manuelo, that was so totally great!" Riley cried, giving him a hug.

Chloe came up and hugged him, too. "I didn't know you could do all that stuff! You really are amazing!"

"I think I'm definitely getting an A." Riley laughed. "Thank you, Manuelo! I don't know what I would have done without you!"

The bell rang, and everyone headed out. Riley was still smiling as she left. But then Willow rushed to catch up to her.

"Guess what?" Willow asked.

"Why don't you just tell me?" Riley snapped.

"You mean you're not in the mood for guessing games?" Willow laughed. "Okay. Alex's band is rehearsing tonight, and I'm going to be there."

So am I, Riley started to say. But she suddenly remembered—she couldn't go to The Wave's rehearsal tonight. She had to stay home because of the family portrait!

"Guess what?" Riley told her. "I don't care where you go." But she didn't mean it. She didn't mean it at all.

"Chloe...Riley!" Macy Carlson called up from the living room that evening. "The photographer's here!"

Riley checked herself in the mirror in her bedroom. Her yellow top, back from the dry cleaner, looked great.

She smoothed her hair and turned to Chloe. "Ready?"

"Almost." Chloe tugged at the sleeves of her blue sweater.

"Let's hurry and get this over with," Riley said. "I want to get to the band rehearsal before Willow hooks her claws into Alex."

"Okay, okay," Chloe said, peering into the mirror. "I'm not in the mood for this, either, you know. I'd rather be with Travis."

"Did you have a date?" Riley asked.

"No, but we could have," Chloe said. "Well, if he'd asked me. And if he'd asked me, I would have had to say no."

Riley was a little confused, but before she could say anything, their mother called again. Riley and her sister hurried downstairs to the living room, where the photographer was setting up her tripod and camera.

"Good, you're here," Macy said. She gestured toward the photographer. "This is Janice Taylor. Do what she says and she'll make us all look great."

Ms. Taylor nodded and made some adjustments to her camera.

"You already look great, Dad," Riley said. "Is that a new tie?"

Her father smoothed down his blue tie. "I bought it just for this occasion," he said. "You like it?"

"It's a little pale," Macy remarked.

"Well, I was kind of hoping he'd wear the tie I gave him for Father's Day," Chloe chimed in.

Riley rolled her eyes. "Why would he wear that? It's green and has D*ad* written all over it."

"So? It *is* a family photo," Chloe argued.

Macy shook her head. "A nice deep red tie would look better."

"I like *this* one," Jake declared.

The photographer clapped her hands. "Okay, people, could we finish the family argument *after* the family photo?" She pointed to the couch. "Girls, you two sit in the middle with Mom and Dad on either end."

Chloe, Riley, and their parents seated themselves and faced the camera. "Wait," Chloe said. "We're missing somebody. Pepper, where are you? Come on, Pepper!"

Tail wagging, the dog trotted into the room. Around her neck was a wide purple ribbon tied in a big bow.

"Pepper, you look so cute!" Chloe exclaimed.

Riley scooped the dog onto the couch between her and Chloe.

The photographer peered through the lens. "Very nice. Squeeze a little closer together."

As they shifted closer, Manuelo walked into the room wearing a charcoal-gray suit, a starched white shirt, and a yellow silk tie.

"Whoa, Manuelo, you look so nice!" Riley said.

"Yeah, what's the big occasion?" Jake asked.

"Smile and hold it, everybody," the photographer said.

Everyone froze as the flash went off.

Jake blinked a few times and looked at Manuelo again. "What's the occasion?" he repeated.

Manuelo raised his eyebrows. "Well, I thought *this* was the big occasion. A family portrait," he said. "I assumed I was part of the family. I guess I was wrong."

Oh, no! Riley thought. We left him out. We didn't mean to, but we did! "But, Manuelo—" she began.

"No," Manuelo interrupted her. "It's clear to me now. Although I have served you all for fourteen years as a nanny, housecleaner, cook, counselor, and confidant, I am still only a domestic to you." He looked at Riley and Chloe. "One who got a standing ovation, I might add."

Riley felt her face flush with guilt.

"A what?" Jake asked.

Manuelo ignored him and strode to the front door. "So, since I am considered only an employee, I will do as employees do. I quit!"

Before anyone could say a word, Manuelo opened the door and walked out.

chapter
seven

Chloe couldn't move. No one else could either. They all stared at the door, totally stunned.

Then Chloe raced across the room, yanked open the door, and looked outside. The taillights of Manuelo's car were just disappearing around the corner.

"He's gone!" Chloe cried, running back into the living room. "He's really gone!"

"I think I'll leave, too," the photographer murmured. No one paid any attention as she packed up her equipment and slipped out the door.

Macy turned to Jake. "I can't believe you asked him what the big occasion was. Could you be any more thoughtless?"

"Me? You organized the picture," Jake protested. "You're the one who left him out of it."

"No," Chloe said. "We *all* left him out of it."

Riley nodded. "It's everybody's fault."

"You're right," Macy agreed, pacing the room. "I think of him as a member of the family, but do I treat him like one? No. And after all he does for us—the cooking and cleaning and..." She paused and frowned at the girls. "By the way, what did he mean about getting a standing ovation?"

[**Chloe**: I was kind of hoping nobody heard that. But Mom doesn't miss much, even in a crisis. And since it was my idea to keep it a secret, I guess I'm the one who should confess.]

"Here's the thing," Chloe said. "Riley and I had to invite people to our business studies class for Career Week. You know, to talk about their jobs and stuff."

"Why didn't you ask *me*?" Mrs. Carlson said.

"Or me?" Jake asked.

"Well, Dad, you don't exactly have a job," Chloe reminded him. "And we were afraid we'd hurt your feelings if we left you out."

"So Chloe invited Tedi, and I asked Manuelo," Riley explained.

"And I talked Riley into keeping it a secret so we wouldn't hurt *both* your feelings," Chloe said. "But anyway, who cares about that now? Manuelo's gone!"

"You should have seen him in class," Riley said. "He was totally awesome. He cooked, and he gave Miss Westmore a makeover, and everybody loved him.... I feel so guilty!"

Macy nodded sadly. "So do I."

"Me, too," Chloe murmured, trying to swallow the lump in her throat. "Poor Manuelo."

"Now wait. There's no sense in falling apart," Jake declared. "Manuelo hasn't gone for good."

Chloe sniffed. "How can you be so sure?"

"Because he left everything behind," Jake explained. "He didn't even take any clothes with him."

"That's right!" Chloe agreed. She started to feel a tiny bit better. "He'll have to come back. And when he does, we'll make everything up to him!"

The next morning Chloe hurried into the kitchen eager to see if Manuelo was back. But Mom was at the counter packing lunches for school and Riley was digging into a box of Kellogg's Pop-Tarts.

Chloe knew she didn't need to ask, but she did anyway. "He didn't come back, did he?"

Riley shook her head. Sitting at her feet, Pepper kept her eyes on the box of pastries. "I checked his room," Riley said glumly. "All his clothes and everything are still there. I'm so worried. I mean, where did he sleep?"

"I'm sure he went to a friend's," Macy said.

"Right," Chloe said, relieved. She thought for a second. "Who *are* his friends, anyway?"

Riley thought for a moment, too. Then she shook her head. "I don't know."

"Me, either," Chloe admitted. "That's so terrible! I mean, Manuelo knows all our friends, and I've never even asked about his. I don't know a single name!"

"I know a few of them," Macy said. "I'm going to try to find Manuelo's address book. Chloe, while I'm gone, would you make some coffee? I'm barely awake."

"I can tell. That's a raw egg you put into my lunch bag," Riley told her. "Chloe, what kind of Pop-Tart do you want for breakfast—strawberry or chocolate?"

"Neither," Chloe replied. "And forget the egg, Mom. I don't even like hard-boiled ones."

As Macy headed for Manuelo's room, Riley tore open a pastry. She fed a bite to Pepper, then put the rest of it down. "I'm feeling too guilty to eat."

"So am I." Chloe filled the coffeepot with water and poured it into the machine. After a little searching, she found a bag of coffee in the refrigerator and dumped some into the filter. When she heard the back door open, she spun around. "Manuelo?" she cried hopefully.

Jake stepped inside. "It's just me."

"Oh. Hi, Dad," Chloe said, turning on the coffee machine. "Sorry about that. I didn't mean to sound so disappointed."

"That's okay, honey," he said. "I just wanted to stop by and see if he was back. I guess he's not, huh?"

"Mom's getting his address book so she can call some of his friends," Riley said.

"His address book isn't in his room," Macy announced,

coming back into the kitchen. "It must have been in his jacket. I'll look up the numbers in the regular phone book in a second." She poured herself some coffee, took a sip, and almost choked. "Chloe, what did you do to this? It's as thick as mud!"

"Well, I can't help it!" Chloe burst out. "I've never made coffee. Manuelo always does it!"

"I know. I'm sorry," Macy said. "I'm just mad at myself. I never realized how much I take Manuelo for granted."

"We all do," Jake said.

Riley nodded. "I never even thanked him for getting my blouse dry-cleaned. Or fixing my hair dryer. Or—"

The phone rang. Riley dived for it. "Manuelo?"

Chloe watched her sister's face fall. Not Manuelo, she thought.

Riley held out the phone. "It's for you, Mom. Something about a shipment of fabric."

As Macy took the phone, Jake turned to the girls. "I'll finish the lunches. You two get ready for school."

"I don't feel like going to school," Chloe said as she and Riley trudged up to their room. "I'm just going to worry about Manuelo all day."

"Me, too. But I'll call home between classes in case something happens," Riley said. She stopped suddenly, pointing to the backpack on her bed. "Oh, no—look!"

Chloe stared at the bag. "What's wrong with it?"

"Nothing—*now*," Riley replied, her lower lip quivering. "Because Manuelo fixed it for me."

"I remember," Chloe said softly. "He always does stuff for us, even when we don't ask." She wandered over to the dresser to brush her hair and almost burst into tears when she saw the snapshot of Manuelo stuck in the mirror frame. "Remember this?" she said, tapping the photograph. "Manuelo in his Halloween costume."

"Yeah. He was Peter Pan." Riley smiled a little. "Or was it the Jolly Green Giant?"

Chloe's eyes filled with tears. "We don't have many photos of him, and you know why? Because *he* took most of the family pictures!" she wailed.

"Chloe, don't!" Riley pleaded. "This won't help us find Manuelo. And that's what we have to do. So we need a plan."

Chloe sniffed and wiped her eyes. "Okay. A plan...a plan..." She glanced at the photo of Manuelo again. "We could show his picture around school and ask everybody to keep an eye out for him."

"Good!" Riley thought for a moment. "And we can make a list of the places he goes all the time. We can go around to them after school and ask them to call us if he comes in."

"Right. And who knows? We might even see him!" Chloe took the snapshot from the mirror and tucked it into her bag. Having a plan made her feel a little better. She just hoped it worked.

chapter eight

"**H**ave you seen this man?" Standing at her locker, Chloe thrust Manuelo's photograph in front of Blake Johnson, a guy from her English class.

Blake stopped and peered at the photo. "Whoa! What *is* that—a frog costume?"

"No, it's a... Never mind," Chloe said. "Look at his face. Have you seen him, like, since last night?"

Blake shook his head. "Nope. Sorry. Who is he?"

Chloe started to say he was their housekeeper but changed her mind. "He's part of my family," she said. "If you see him, tell me, okay?"

"Sure. Hope you find him," Blake said as he walked away.

"Thanks." Chloe sighed. She'd been roaming the halls before homeroom, showing Manuelo's picture around. So far, no one had seen him.

She checked her watch. Only a few more minutes

until class. She slammed her locker and spotted Amanda waving to her from down the hall. Clutching the photograph, she hurried toward her. "Amanda, have you seen Manuelo?" she asked.

"Not since I was at your house last week," Amanda said. "Why? What's going on?"

Chloe quickly told her what had happened. "Riley and I really need to find him," she said. "If you see him, tell me, okay?"

"Absolutely," Amanda agreed.

"Thanks, Amanda. See you at lunch." Chloe gave her friend a wave and sped back down the hall. As she rounded the corner, she bumped into Larry.

"Hi, Chloe," Larry said. "Is Riley around?"

"Sure. Somewhere," Chloe told him. "Listen, Larry, have you seen Manuelo?"

"Is this a trick question?" Larry asked, sounding suspicious. "I mean, I live next door, so naturally I've seen—"

"Larry! I'm totally serious," Chloe said, and she told him what had happened.

Larry shook his head. "I haven't seen him since business studies class yesterday at Career Week. He was really excellent!"

Chloe sighed. This plan wasn't working out after all. Actually, now that she thought about it, it never was a very good plan to begin with. But she couldn't think of anything else.

"Well, if you see him, *please* tell me. I'm going to keep showing around his picture." Chloe held up the snapshot.

Larry scowled at it. "I hate to tell you, Chloe, but it's almost impossible to identify Manuelo from that picture. He looks like a turtle."

"It was Halloween, and he was the Jolly Green Giant," Chloe said defensively. "Or maybe Peter Pan."

"Whatever," Larry said. "Anyway, it doesn't look like him. Why don't you use a drawing?"

"Because I don't have one," Chloe said. "Besides, I can't draw very well, and neither can Riley."

"I have a little artistic talent," Larry declared, ducking his head and pretending to be modest. "I'll do a drawing for you."

"You will? Thanks, Larry!" Chloe said. "Then Riley and I can make copies and hand them out to people and stick them up all over town."

"Hey! Do you think this will help my chances with Riley?" Larry asked hopefully.

"Larry!"

"Just kidding," he said. "I know Manuelo's like family. I'll do a sketch during study hall and give it to you this afternoon. Let me have the picture."

As Chloe thanked him again, Travis rounded the corner. Chloe's heart thumped as he ambled toward her, a lazy smile on his face. "Hi. What's up?" he asked.

"Manuelo's missing," Larry told him.

Travis looked blank. "Who?"

"Manuelo," Chloe repeated, pointing to the photo she'd just handed to Larry. "You met him at my house a few weeks ago, remember?"

"Oh, right. Your housekeeper." Travis glanced at the photograph. "Is that really him?"

"I know, it's a terrible picture," Chloe said.

"Which I'm going to fix." Larry slid the photo into his shirt pocket and headed down the hall.

"Thanks, Larry. I'll never forget this," Chloe called after him. "Neither will Riley!"

"So what happened?" Travis asked as he and Chloe began walking together. "Did the guy not show up for work or something?"

"Manuelo? Well, sort of. But it's way more compli-cated than that." As Chloe started to explain, the warn-ing bell rang. "Never mind. I'll tell you later."

"Sure. Why don't you come over after school and hang out?" Travis suggested.

[Chloe: Don't you hate it when something you wish for actually happens, and it's the wrong time? I mean, if we hung out more, we'd auto-matically get closer, right?]

"I'd really love to, Travis, but I can't," Chloe said. "I have to look for Manuelo after school. I have to find him."

"Well...okay." Travis looked a little disappointed.

Chloe was disappointed, too. Then she realized

there was an easy way to fix this. "Why don't you come with me?" she suggested. "Larry's doing a sketch of Manuelo, and I'm going to make copies and put them up all over the place."

"Well, I kind of thought we could play video games or something," he said. "Can't you just come over?"

Chloe was amazed. Video games? Didn't he hear what she just said? "Travis, Manuelo is very important to me. I can't come over today. I have to look for him. Do you want to help me or not?"

Chloe stared at him, waiting for an answer. Actually, she stared at the tiny red pimple emerging on the left side of his nose.

"Well...okay. I guess we can put up the pictures." He smiled at her.

Chloe smiled back. Good answer, she thought. She was beginning to think that Travis didn't care about her feelings. And for once Chloe was glad to be wrong.

Riley stuffed some coins into the pay phone by the principal's office and quickly punched in her home number. Business studies class started in less than a minute, but she didn't care if she was late. She had to find out if Manuelo was home.

Mom picked up on the first ring. "Manuelo?" she asked breathlessly.

"No, Mom, it's me, Riley." Riley's shoulders slumped. "He's not back, huh?"

"Not yet." Macy sighed. "Your father's out driving around, looking for him."

"Okay. I have to go now," Riley said. "I'll call later." She hung up, dashed through the halls, and arrived at class just as the bell rang.

"Meet me at my locker after history," Chloe said as Riley passed her desk. "Larry's doing a drawing of Manuelo, and I'm making copies for us to put up."

"Great." Riley hurried down the aisle, sat down, and pulled a notebook from her backpack.

Willow entered the room with an attractive woman wearing a blue suit and a confident expression.

Riley groaned to herself. The woman was Willow's Career Week speaker—Alex's mother.

[Riley: Look at the way Mrs. Zimmer is smiling at Willow. It's so obvious she likes her. Manuelo's gone, and I have to sit through this! Could the day be any worse?]

As Willow passed Riley's desk, she quickly leaned over and whispered, "I had a great time at the band rehearsal!"

Willow breezed on by, and Riley frowned. Thanks for reminding me, Willow, she thought. Once Manuelo left, she totally forgot about The Wave's rehearsal.

Willow stood in front of the class and gestured to Alex's mom. "This is Alison Zimmer. She was elected to the town council last year. I'm interested in politics, so she was the first person I thought of for Career Week."

Ha! Riley thought. Willow's interested in Alex, not politics.

"I'm really grateful that she could come because she's so busy," Willow went on. "I didn't realize being on the town council was so much work! But I guess I'll get a chance to find out what it's like for myself—I'm going to be working for her over the summer!"

[Riley: I can't even look at Willow up there. I know she's smiling at me. And do you know why? Because Alex will be working in his mom's office, too. He and Willow are going to spend the whole summer together!]

As Alex's mother began to speak, Riley opened her notebook. Instead of taking notes, however, she started making a list of places in town where Manuelo went all the time.

She couldn't do anything about the summer job situation. But she *could* work on the search for Manuelo. She'd just have to worry about Willow later.

Right now, finding Manuelo was the most important thing.

chapter
nine

"Okay, I've got a list," Riley declared at Chloe's locker later that day. "Supermarket, health food store, dry cleaner, gym, video place, barber shop, gas station."

"Don't forget the frozen yogurt shops," Chloe reminded her. "Manuelo eats tons of it."

"Right." Riley got out a pen and was adding the names when Larry arrived.

"Hi, Riley! I've got the sketch," he announced, holding out a sheet of paper. "What do you think?"

It was definitely Manuelo, Riley thought, looking at the sketch. Dark hair, a little thin on top. Friendly brown eyes. The corners of his mouth turning up as if he was about to break into a grin.

Riley felt a lump in her throat. She glanced at Chloe and saw a tear in her eye. "Oh, Larry!" Riley said.

"You don't like it?" he asked. "You're right. I got the eyes too close together. Listen, I'll try again."

"No, it's perfect!" Chloe cried.

"It really is," Riley agreed. "You even remembered that he's starting to go bald on top."

"Just looking at it makes me miss him even more," Chloe choked out.

Riley nodded sadly. "Me, too."

Larry sniffed. "He was a good friend to us all."

"Okay, wait." Riley got hold of herself. "Manuelo's not dead. He's only missing. We can't stand around blubbering about it. We have to find him."

"You're right." Chloe took a deep breath. "I'll go make a bunch of copies of the sketch."

"I already did," Larry announced. He pulled a thick stack of papers from his backpack. "Ta da!"

"Thanks, Larry!" Chloe kissed his cheek, and Riley was so grateful she found herself giving him a hug. Larry walked off looking dazed and totally happy.

Riley and Chloe each took half the sketches and headed in different directions. Riley decided to go by the principal's office and call home again before her next class. This time her father answered.

"No word from Manuelo," Jake reported. "I'm going on a grocery run for your mother, and I'll keep an eye out. Try not to worry, honey. He hasn't been gone even a whole day yet."

Dad was right, Riley thought as she hung up. Manuelo hadn't been gone that long. But he'd been so totally furious, she couldn't help worrying. What if he never forgave them? What if Manuelo never came back?

Leaving the pay phone, Riley passed a bulletin board and stopped to tack up a sketch. Across the bottom, she wrote *missing*! and her home phone number for people to call.

"Riley, hi," Sierra said, coming up to her as Riley finished writing her message. "I guess you haven't found him yet, huh?"

Riley shook her head. She'd told Sierra about Manuelo earlier. "Chloe and I are going to put these up around town after school."

"Good idea. Want me to put some up, too?" Sierra offered.

"Sure! Thanks." Riley gave her several sketches. "By the way, you'll never guess what Willow did."

"Uh-oh. Now what?" Sierra demanded.

Riley told her about Willow getting a job with Alex's mother. "Can you believe it? She'll be with him practically every day!"

"Very tricky. Cozy, too," Sierra added.

"Don't remind me." Riley groaned. "I wish I could talk to Manuelo about this. I wonder if he'd still tell me not to say anything to Alex."

"Speaking of Alex," Sierra said, pointing down the hall, "there he is now. Gotta go. Call me later, okay?" With a quick wave to Alex, Sierra sped off.

"Hey," Alex said, coming up to Riley. "Did Sierra tell you we canceled band practice today?"

Riley shook her head, still trying to decide whether to bring up the Willow topic.

"Well, Marta's sick," Alex explained.

"I guess it's hard to practice without keyboards," Riley said.

Alex nodded. "So do you want to do something after school?"

Yes! Riley thought. A chance to be together! Without Willow, which was really important. But finding Manuelo was just as important.

"I'd really like to, Alex, but I can't," Riley said reluctantly. She showed him the sketch of Manuelo and told him what was going on. "I'm going to put up more of his pictures in town after school. I want to do something with you, but…"

"Hey, no problem," Alex told her. "I'll come with you and help."

"You will?" Yes! Riley thought again. Take that, Willow!

Alex nodded. "So I'll meet you after school, and we'll try to find Manuelo." Alex leaned close and gave Riley a quick kiss. "See you later. Oh—your hair looks great, by the way."

"It does?" Riley asked, surprised. She'd been so worried about Manuelo this morning, she'd barely looked in the mirror. Had she even brushed her hair?

"You're wearing it down again," Alex said. "I really like it that way."

Riley smiled, feeling totally thrilled. "Thanks, Alex."

[<u>Riley</u>: I know what you're thinking. Manuelo told me my hair looked better down, so I should be thanking him, right? Well, I will—as soon as I find him!]

The girl behind the counter at Malibu Yogurt shook her head. "I haven't seen him since last week," she said, handing the sketch of Manuelo back to Riley. "He got a banana-berry smoothie. That's his favorite."

"Are you sure it was last week?" Riley asked.

"Positive. He hasn't been in since," the girl declared. "Well, not on my shift, anyway. I only work afternoons, and the store's open from nine to nine."

"I didn't think of that," Riley said. "I guess I'll have to come back."

"Can we put the sketch up in the window?" Alex asked the girl.

"Sure, go ahead," she said. "I hope you find him. He's a really nice guy."

"He's great," Riley agreed with a sigh. "Thanks."

"Don't feel too down," Alex said as he and Riley left the shop. "We've only been to four stores so far."

"I know," Riley said. "It's just that everybody we've talked to says what a great guy Manuelo is. And they're right. It makes me feel even more guilty."

"So when you find him, you'll apologize." Alex squeezed her hand. "Hey, I can't believe we left that place without getting a cone. Want one?"

"Sure. Chocolate swirl with sprinkles," Riley said. "Thanks."

As Alex dashed back into the frozen yogurt shop, Riley glanced around and spotted her sister coming down the sidewalk. "Chloe, hi!" she called. "What are you doing here?"

"Same thing you are," Chloe said, tapping the pile of sketches she was holding. She peered through the shop window. "Is that Alex?"

Riley nodded. "He wanted to come with me and help."

"Really? I asked Travis to help, and he said okay." Chloe looked a little glum. "You haven't seen him around, have you?"

Riley shook her head. She wondered what Travis's problem was. He was almost always late. Sometimes he didn't show up at all. And why did Chloe have to ask him to help, anyway? Why didn't he offer, like Alex?

"I guess we could have missed each other after school," Chloe said.

"Sure," Riley agreed. Actually, she wasn't sure at all, but Chloe needed cheering up. "Maybe he's looking for you now."

Chloe's expression brightened a little. "Right. Okay, I'll keep going. Say hi to Alex."

After Chloe left, Alex emerged with two chocolate cones, both with sprinkles. Riley was just taking her first bite when Alex said, "Look, there's Willow!"

[Riley: You probably didn't think it was possible
to choke on yogurt, right? Well, take my word for
it, it is.]

"Hi, you guys," Willow said, walking up to Riley and
Alex. "Riley, are you okay?"

"Uh...uh..." Riley coughed. How did Willow always
find them, anyway? Did she plant some secret tracking
device in Alex's backpack? "Uh...I'm okay," she finally
managed to choke out.

"Are you sure?" Willow asked. "Your face is totally red."

Thanks for pointing that out, Willow, Riley thought.
"I'm fine. What are you doing here, Willow?" she asked.

Alex gave her a funny look. Riley realized how sharp
she'd sounded, so she coughed some more. "Frog in my
throat," she croaked.

Willow held up a bag from the card shop. "I needed
to buy a thank-you card for Alex's mom."

How sweet, Riley thought. Now how do I get rid of her?

Before Riley could think of a way, Alex started
telling Willow about Manuelo. "Riley made a list of the
stores he goes to and we're trying to hit them all."

"Yeah, and we'd better keep going," Riley said, lick-
ing some yogurt. "We still have a ton of places to check.
See you, Willow."

"Mind if I walk with you guys?" Willow asked as Riley
and Alex started down the sidewalk.

"Sure, come on," Alex told her.

Willow gave Riley a triumphant smile, and Riley felt

Willow had planned, Riley thought, still seething. Maybe Willow *was* winning. Maybe by this time next , Alex would be Willow's boyfriend instead of /'s.

I can't let that happen, Riley said silently. I have to omething. Keeping quiet is definitely not working!

Suddenly, Riley realized she was walking alone. She ied around and saw Willow leaning close to Alex, iling as she murmured something to him.

Alex murmured something back and laughed.

Willow threw an arm around his shoulders and gave n a hug. When she saw Riley watching, she grinned. lex is great, isn't he? I'm starting to remember how uch fun we had together. Better watch out, Riley!"

Alex laughed again. So did Willow.

But Riley's temper had finally reached the boiling oint. She couldn't hold back any longer. "This isn't a ike, Alex!" she burst out angrily. "Willow really meant vhat she just said!"

"What? No, I didn't," Willow protested. "I was only idding."

Alex looked confused. "Riley, what are you talking about?"

"Why don't you tell him the truth?" Riley said to Willow. "You want him back!"

Alex glanced at Willow.

Willow rolled her eyes.

"Go ahead, Willow, admit it," Riley declared.

like screaming. This was getting to be w

Fuming inside, Riley walked down t
the next shop on her list, the dry cleaner
window said: NO FOOD, DRINK, OR BARE FEET.

"I'll hold your cone while you go i
Willow offered.

Riley had no choice. Gritting her teeth,
over her yogurt and went inside, leaving Ale
Willow.

The owner knew Manuelo, but he hadn'
recently. He took one of the sketches, promis
it in the window. Riley thanked him and hurrie

Willow and Alex were sitting together on a
bench. Very close together, Riley noticed.

She barely remembered what she said to the c
All she knew was that, from the window, she saw v
laugh and touch Alex on the arm. Then Alex gave
a bite of his cone. He wiped a little chocolate off
with a napkin.

"Any luck?" Alex asked as Willow gave Riley b
cone.

Riley shook her head. "Let's keep going."

By the time they'd gone to the health food
two more frozen-yogurt shops and the video store
was discouraged and angry. Nobody had seen Ma
and Willow was still sticking to Alex like glue.

Of course, Alex didn't totally ignore Riley. B
paid plenty of attention to Willow, too. Which is e

Alex stared at her as if she were crazy. "Riley, what's with you lately?" he asked. "You know Willow and I are just good friends. Why are you so jealous?"

As soon as he said that, Riley knew she had made a mistake.

[Riley: See how he's looking at me? He's disappointed. He's even a little mad. Now that he thinks I'm jealous, I can't tell him about the notebook with the hearts. And I can't prove that Willow actually told me she wanted him back. This whole thing is a mess. It's exactly what Manuelo warned me about!]

"Sorry," Riley muttered. "Forget I said anything, please. I'm upset about Manuelo, that's all."

Willow nodded. "Sure. Whatever."

Alex gave Riley a little smile. But he didn't hold her hand as they continued walking, and Riley had the feeling that he wouldn't forget her outburst.

Riley felt like screaming—at herself. Why couldn't she have kept her big mouth shut? And what was she going to do now?

chapter
ten

"**H**ere you go, girls," Jake Carlson said in the kitchen Wednesday morning. He had come over early to check about Manuelo and stayed to make breakfast. He put plates in front of Chloe and Riley. "Pancakes, hot off the griddle!"

"Thanks, Dad." Chloe stared at her plate. The pancakes looked okay, but she wasn't hungry. For one thing, she didn't like such a big breakfast. For another, Manuelo still wasn't back. And for a third, what happened to Travis yesterday? She didn't run into him in town, and he wasn't home when she called last night.

Why didn't he meet her like he said he would?

"Eat a few bites or you'll hurt his feelings," Riley whispered as their father refilled Mom's coffee cup.

Chloe nodded. Dad was trying to be helpful. The least she could do was eat a little.

Chloe took a bite. "Uh…"

"I know, the bottoms are burned," Riley whispered. "Just feed the rest to Pepper—she doesn't care."

"Right," Chloe whispered back. She glanced over her shoulder. Dad was at the stove with his back to the table. She picked up a pancake and dropped it to the floor, where Pepper waited hopefully.

Chloe cut up a second pancake and pushed the pieces around her plate. She was worried about Manuelo, but she couldn't help thinking about Travis. She kept trying to figure out why he didn't show up. Did they decide which door to meet at? She couldn't remember. Maybe not. Maybe she waited at the wrong one.

With another quick look at Dad, Chloe dropped some pieces of pancake to the floor.

Riley fed the dog the last of her breakfast and took her plate to the counter. "Hey, Dad, do you think you could drive me to the gym and the gas station after school today? I want to check if Manuelo's been there, and they're too far to walk to."

"Sure, honey. I'll pick you up after school."

"I wish I could come," Macy said, finishing her coffee. "But I better get some work done. It's just so hard to concentrate with Manuelo gone."

"I called more of his friends," Jake said. "Artie Shawn and Kerra Simpson. They haven't seen him. Dave Michaels is out of town, but he'll be back tonight. I'll try then."

Or Travis could have gotten out of class late, Chloe

thought. So he looked for her in town but couldn't find her. Maybe they totally missed each other. Maybe.

A figure suddenly appeared in the hall doorway.

"Larry!" Chloe cried. "You scared me. What are you doing in the house?"

Larry grinned nervously, his eyes shifting back and forth. "I...uh..."

"He came to see Riley—what else?" Mom said.

"Yeah—Riley!" Larry quickly agreed. "That's right, I came to see if she wanted to walk to school with me."

"Yeah, but why didn't you come in the kitchen door the way you always do?" Chloe asked.

"I did! I mean, I knocked!" Larry declared.

"You never knock," Chloe pointed out.

"There's always a first time," Larry told her. "Anyway, I guess you guys didn't hear me. So I came in the front door. Sorry if I scared you, Chloe. See you!"

Larry hurried away. A few seconds later the front door slammed.

"Is it just me, or was Larry acting weird?" Chloe asked.

"It's just you," Riley replied, rinsing off her plate.

"No, something's up with him," Chloe said. "He didn't wait to see if you'd walk with him."

Riley rolled her eyes. "Well, I'm not complaining."

Chloe shrugged and took her plate to the sink. She had too much on her mind to worry about Larry. He *was* acting weird, but, after all, that was hardly a news flash.

● ● ●

At school, Chloe sat through her morning classes with an intent, thoughtful expression on her face. She had the look down perfectly, and the teachers thought she was paying attention. So she was free to think about other things.

Manuelo was her biggest worry, but Travis kept nudging his way into her thoughts. She kept trying to push him out. After all, wasn't it selfish to be thinking about boy problems when Manuelo was still gone?

Definitely selfish, Chloe decided.

"I just can't help being disappointed about yesterday," she told Amanda as they walked to the cafeteria together.

"I don't blame you," Amanda said.

"I'm sure we just missed each other."

Amanda frowned. "Then why didn't he call? You're making excuses for him."

Am I? Chloe wondered. I don't want to make excuses. I want Travis to be there for me the way Alex is for Riley. But I can't get mad yet. I have to find out what happened.

"There he is," Chloe said as they entered the cafeteria. "I'm going to talk to him. I'll meet you at the table."

Waving good-bye to Amanda, Chloe hurried across the room. "Hey, Travis."

"You're just in time," he said with a smile. "I'm a quarter short. Mind if I borrow one?"

"Sure. I missed you yesterday," she said, fishing around in her backpack. "After school, I mean."

"Right. Sorry about that," Travis said as she handed him a quarter. "I forgot."

[<u>Chloe</u>: **Forgot? How could he forget me? I'm supposed to be his girlfriend!**]

"Then, when I remembered, I waited for a while, but you must have already gone," Travis went on, pushing four quarters into the soda machine.

Chloe didn't know what to think. Forgetting was bad, but then again, he did remember eventually. Was that good enough?

Chloe stared at him, trying to decide. The only thing she was sure about was that that tiny pimple by his nose was getting bigger. In fact, he was getting another one above his right eyebrow. Well, nobody's perfect, she thought.

Travis punched a button, and a Coke thumped down. "I was going to call you last night, but I had a bunch of things to do." He popped the top on the Coke and took a drink. "Anyway, how about today? Want to hang after school?"

"I can't," Chloe told him. "I have to go to more places and put up Manuelo's picture. He still hasn't come back. I might be able to come over later," she added hopefully.

Travis shook his head. "I'll be at Kyle's. We're going to overhaul the engine on his bike."

"Oh. Well, maybe tomorrow," Chloe said. Then she

had an idea. "Listen, I just thought of something. Since you guys are always riding around on your bikes, maybe you could put up some of Manuelo's pictures for me."

"Sure, I guess we could do that." Travis frowned as Chloe took a few sketches from her backpack. "But I don't get it. Why don't you just hire a new housekeeper?"

Was he kidding? Chloe wondered. No, he was totally serious. Well, he just didn't understand, that was all. "Manuelo's not just a housekeeper. He's part of the family," she explained. "Even if we hired somebody else, we'd still want Manuelo back."

Travis raised his hands in the air. "Okay, okay. I get it, Chloe."

Did he? Chloe wondered. She hoped so.

"Hi, Riley." Sierra sat down next to Riley on the front steps of the school. She'd changed into her "at home" look—neat ponytail, blouse, and knee-length skirt. "School's over. How come you're just sitting here?"

"I'm waiting for my dad," Riley said. "We're going to drive around and put up more pictures of Manuelo." Riley sighed. "I wish he'd come home."

"I bet he will," Sierra said. "Listen, have you talked to Alex today?"

Riley groaned. She'd already told Sierra about yesterday's Willow disaster. "I only saw him for a couple of minutes this morning. And he didn't act the same. I think he's still embarrassed. Or mad...Why?" she asked, suddenly suspicious. "Did he say something to you?"

Sierra shook her head. "I just wondered. Uh-oh. Willow alert." She pointed toward another set of doors at the end of the building.

Willow was just coming out. And behind her—close behind her—was Alex.

"They're together!" Riley whispered, even though she knew they couldn't hear her. "Again."

"Don't freak," Sierra whispered back.

Riley watched tensely as Alex and Willow began walking. "I can't stand it! I blew up yesterday, and now Alex would rather be with Willow. Her plan is working!"

"I don't believe it," Sierra said. "Alex wouldn't dump you overnight."

Riley kept watching. Willow's backpack slid off her shoulder and as she picked it up, she glanced toward where Riley and Sierra were sitting.

For a split second, Willow gazed at Riley. Riley spotted a smirk on the girl's face before she turned back to Alex.

When Willow hoisted her bag onto her shoulder, she accidentally bumped Alex. He staggered, laughing. Willow laughed, too, then slipped an arm around his shoulders in a playful hug.

"She did that on purpose," Riley muttered.

"Why don't you go after them?" Sierra urged her. "He's *your* boyfriend."

"You know, you're right," Riley agreed. "I'll show up

the way she always does and see how she likes it!"

As Riley jumped to her feet, her father pulled up in the car.

"Hi, honey," Jake called out the window. "Are you ready?"

Riley glanced at Alex and Willow. Finding Manuelo comes first, she reminded herself.

"Let's go, Dad," she said and hurried toward the car.

chapter
eleven

"Why don't you wait for Mom to do that?" Riley suggested as Chloe scooped coffee into the machine Thursday morning. "Mom likes coffee, not sludge."

"Very funny. Mom was waiting for Dad to make it because she likes his better than hers," Chloe replied. "But Dad called before you came down and he won't be over until later, so I decided to do it. I watched Dad yesterday. Five cups of water, five scoops of coffee. That was two."

As Chloe transferred the third scoop of coffee to the filter, a sudden shriek rang out. Chloe jumped, slinging ground coffee all over the counter. "What was that?"

"I think it was Mom," Riley said, jumping up from the table. "Mom, are you okay?" she shouted.

Footsteps sounded in the hall, and Macy Carlson burst into the kitchen. "He was here!" she announced, a devastated expression on her face.

"Who? Manuelo?" Chloe cried.

"What do you mean, *was*?" Riley asked.

Macy took a shaky breath. "I went into his room," she said. "I thought I might find *some* kind of clue to where he went…and some of his clothes are missing!"

"Are you sure?" Chloe asked.

Macy nodded. "When I was in there Tuesday, two shirts were draped over the back of his chair. And so was his bird-of-paradise tie. You know the one."

Riley nodded. "I always teased him about that tie," she said sadly.

"Hey!" Chloe cried, "I bought him that for his birthday last year. It's a great tie!"

"Well, it's gone," Macy declared. "The tie and the shirts. And some of his socks, I think. The sock drawer was open."

"So he really was here," Riley said. "But when?"

"I suppose it could have been at any time, except during the day yesterday," Macy said. "I didn't go into his room, but I was here all day. Maybe he came during the night."

Riley glanced at Chloe. "Are you thinking what I'm thinking?"

Chloe nodded. "If Manuelo sneaked in and took his things without leaving a note or anything, it means he doesn't want to see us!" Tears pricked at her eyes. "He's really gone for good!"

• • •

"What are we going to do now?" Chloe asked as she and Riley walked to Riley's locker later that day. "I mean, even if we find Manuelo, he might not want to come back!"

"We still have to find him," Riley declared, opening her locker. "We have to apologize."

"But what if he won't even speak to us?" Chloe asked. "That would be so awful!"

"I know, but we have to try," Riley insisted. She leaned into her locker, searching for a book. "We can't give up, Chloe."

"You're right," Chloe agreed. Leaning against the next locker, she glanced down the hall and spotted Larry coming toward them. She waved at him. "Hi, Larry."

Larry stopped so quickly, his sneakers squeaked. He stared at Chloe for a second, his face turning bright red. Then he slowly walked up to the locker.

"What's the matter with you?" Chloe asked.

"Me? Nothing!" Larry protested. "I'm fine. Great! Couldn't be better!"

Weird, Chloe thought. Weirder than usual, anyway. Larry didn't even say hi to Riley, which he *always* does.

"Listen, I have to go," Larry said, starting to walk away.

Chloe spotted something hanging out of his backpack.

"Larry!" she cried. "You've got something—"

Larry spun around, startled. "What?"

Chloe gasped when she realized what was sticking out of his backpack. An electric-blue necktie. One with huge birds-of-paradise all over it. Manuelo's tie!

[Chloe: Okay, so maybe the tie was a little tackier than I remembered.]

"Where did you get that?" she demanded.

Riley quickly slammed her locker and looked at the tie. "That's Manuelo's!" she cried.

"Huh? No, it's mine." Larry stuffed the tie all the way into his bag. "My grandmother gave it to me a long time ago. See you!"

Chloe narrowed her eyes at Larry as he scurried away. "He's lying," she said to Riley.

"But why did he take Manuelo's tie?" Riley asked.

Chloe wasn't sure. The only thing she could think of was…"Do you think he saw Manuelo?" she asked Riley. "Maybe Manuelo asked Larry to get some of his stuff. Larry *has* been acting kind of nervous lately."

"That would mean Larry knows where Manuelo is, the sneak!" Riley cried excitedly. "Let's go make him spill his guts."

"Wait," Chloe said as Riley started away. "I bet Manuelo made Larry promise not to say anything. He's going to stick to that grandmother story no matter what."

"Okay, but what should we do?" Riley asked.

Chloe thought a second. "We out-sneak him," she

replied. "This is Larry we're talking about, remember? How hard can it be?"

As soon as school was over, Riley and Chloe hurried through the halls and stashed themselves around the corner from Larry's locker. Riley checked her watch. "The bell rang half a minute ago," she said, still breathless from running. "He couldn't have gotten here before us."

"There he is!" Chloe whispered, jumping out of sight.

Riley cautiously peered around the corner and saw Larry walking toward his locker.

"Don't let him spot you!" Chloe said.

"Don't worry, he's looking at the floor," Riley told her. "Okay, he's at his locker. He's got it open. He's taking out a book and putting it into his backpack...."

"What's he doing now?" Chloe asked.

"Closing his locker. Okay, he's on his way," Riley said. "Let's go!"

Keeping a safe distance behind him, Riley and Chloe followed Larry through the halls and out one of the doors. Once outside, Larry began walking at a quick pace.

"Larry never moves this fast," Chloe said. "I wonder what the big rush is."

"Maybe he forgot to give Manuelo the tie, and Manuelo really wants it," Riley joked. "No, wait. I know where he's going. He has a job, remember?"

"Oh, right. He's going to Neptune's Net, that's all," Chloe said. "But Manuelo wouldn't be there, would he?"

"I don't know. Let's just keep going," Riley said.

Still walking quickly, Larry led them to the beach road, then past a bunch of restaurants. When he reached Neptune's Net, he went around to the back.

Riley and Chloe counted to twenty, then followed. The back door of the restaurant was propped open, and they heard pans rattling and male voices.

Riley crept up to the door and peered around it. Several men were inside, chopping vegetables, stirring things in big pots.

Larry was there, too. He wasn't cooking, of course. He was trying to keep out of everyone's way while he spoke to a man wearing a tall white chef's hat.

The man turned around.

"Manuelo!" Riley whispered.

Chloe poked her in the back. "Let me see!"

Riley moved aside, and Chloe peeked in. "Whoa! He's the chef!" Chloe exclaimed.

"Shh!" Riley pulled her out of sight.

"We found him!" Chloe said excitedly. "Isn't this great? We know where he is!"

Riley nodded. "Now for the hard part. We have to talk him into coming home."

chapter
twelve

When Riley walked into school on Friday morning, she stopped at the bulletin board near the office and looked at the sketch of Manuelo.

We've got you now, she thought. Almost, anyway.

As she took down the sketch, Alex came up beside her. "Hi, Riley."

"Alex, hi." Riley automatically checked the hall for Willow. For once, the girl was nowhere in sight. That should have made her feel great, but it didn't. She was nervous. She didn't know what to say to Alex. Should she apologize for the way she'd acted? Or should she try to convince him Willow wanted him back?

Suddenly she noticed that Alex hadn't said anything else. He was as uncomfortable as she was!

This is not good, she told herself. You have to say something! "Guess what?" she asked, waving the sketch in front of Alex's face. "We found him!"

"Hey, that's great!" Alex said. "Where is he?"

"Working at Neptune's Net." As they started down the hall together, Riley described yesterday's discovery.

"What did he say?" Alex asked. "Is he coming back?"

"He still doesn't know we found him," Riley said. "When Chloe and I told Mom and Dad, we all came up with a plan. We're going to dinner at Neptune's Net tonight to totally surprise him. Then we'll ask him to come home."

But what if he says no? Riley wondered. He had a new job, after all. Did he have a new apartment, too? Had he actually started a whole new life?

"It's really cool that you found him," Alex said. "You'll have to tell me all about the big reunion." He started to turn the corner.

"Would you...I mean, do you want to come?" Riley asked. She crossed her fingers. If he says yes, then I haven't totally ruined things. I still have a chance to do something about Willow. Please say yes, she thought.

"Sure. That'll be fun," Alex agreed. "What time?"

All right! Riley thought. "Seven," she said.

"I'll be there," he promised.

"Great!" And Willow won't, Riley thought.

On her way to the cafeteria, Chloe spotted Travis ambling down the hall toward her. "Hi," she said. "Aren't you going to lunch?"

He shook his head. "I've got to do a make-up lab in biology. I'll catch you later, okay?"

"Okay, but wait," she said as he started to walk off. "I've got good news. We found Manuelo."

"Hey, cool," Travis said. "I bet you're glad."

"I really am," Chloe agreed. "We were so worried!"

Travis grinned. "So does this mean you can hang out with me sometimes now?" he asked.

Wow. He didn't even ask if Manuelo was okay, Chloe realized.

"How about tonight?" Travis asked, slinging an arm around her shoulder.

[Chloe: I should feel great, right? Travis has his arm around me. He asked me to hang out with him. But I'm not totally thrilled. If only he asked about Manuelo. If only he wasn't late all those times. If only I was sure he cared about me.]

Chloe started to say she couldn't see him, then changed her mind. "I have a better idea," she said.

"Better than hanging out?" Travis asked.

"Dinner at Neptune's Net," Chloe told him. And it's your last chance, she thought.

Both Travis and Alex were waiting outside the restaurant when the Carlsons arrived at five minutes to seven. Chloe was a little surprised. She actually thought Travis might not show up. But there he was, looking incredibly cool in a black sweater and jeans, with a tiny gold stud glinting in his ear.

But something is missing, Chloe thought. Then she realized what it was. That fluttery feeling in her stomach was gone. Was that good or bad?

"Is everybody ready?" Jake asked as they gathered at the front door.

"You didn't tell me this was a family thing," Travis murmured to Chloe.

"Do you mind?" she asked.

"No, it's cool. I'm just surprised, that's all." Travis took her hand as Jake opened the door and ushered everyone inside.

Dressed in his red lobster costume, Larry waddled clumsily toward them. "Welcome to—" he started to say. Then he stopped suddenly, and his smile faded. "Uh...oh..." he stammered.

"'Uh-oh' is right," Chloe said.

"Hi, Larry," Riley said. "I guess you're surprised to see us here."

"Uh...well..."

Macy tapped her foot impatiently. "Table for six, please, Larry."

"Six?" Larry squeaked. His gaze darted around nervously. "Um...do you have a reservation?"

"The place doesn't take reservations," Jake replied.

"It doesn't? Oh, right, it doesn't!" Larry dramatically slapped a claw against his forehead, making his antennae wobble. "How could I forget?"

"So how about that table?" Jake asked.

"Well…" Larry paused. "Actually, we're full."

Chloe peered into the dining room, where starfish and seashells hung from nets draped on the walls. The room was crowded but definitely not full. "I see some empty tables," she said.

Larry nodded. "Oh, yeah," he said. "But…you know what?" He lowered his voice. "Don't tell anyone I said this, it might cost me my job, but the lobster isn't really fresh today."

"I don't want lobster, anyway," Chloe said. "I'm thinking shrimp."

"Mussels for me," Jake declared.

"But…" Larry's eyes grew even more panicky.

"Larry, just give us a table," Macy insisted. "Now."

"Well…" Larry sighed in defeat. "Okay. Right this way, please." Plucking six menus from the front desk, Larry reluctantly led them into the dining room. Alex and Travis pushed two tables together, and everyone sat down.

Larry handed out the menus, then hurried off to greet more customers.

"Okay, everybody, remember the plan, and just pretend everything's normal," Jake said. He immediately started talking to Macy about her new cruise-wear line.

Travis frowned at Chloe. "What was that supposed to mean?" he asked.

"It's a surprise," she told him. Before Chloe could explain, the waiter arrived to take their orders. Then Alex asked Travis a question about his dirt bike, and the two of them started talking.

Chloe leaned back in her chair, watching the swinging kitchen door.

"Can you see him?" Riley asked.

Chloe shook her head. "The door always closes too fast. He has to be there, though. Look at the way Larry was acting."

"Totally guilty," Riley agreed. "Let's just hope he doesn't warn Manuelo."

"He's pretty busy showing customers in," Chloe told her. "Besides, I don't think Manuelo would leave in the middle of dinner if he's cooking."

In a few more minutes, the waiter arrived with their food. Chloe took a bite of her Shrimp Diablo and quickly put her fork down. "It's definitely his!" she cried. "It's got his secret ingredient. I don't know what it is, but I can taste it!"

"Me, too!" Riley agreed. "Let's go see him now!"

Jake shook his head. "Let's stick to the plan. We finish dinner, then insist on paying our compliments to the chef."

"Okay, but let's eat fast," Riley said.

As Chloe dug into her shrimp dish, Travis nudged her arm. "You want to tell me what's going on now?" he asked.

"That's right, you still don't know," Chloe said. It was hard to believe they had never talked about it. "Okay, remember when I said we found Manuelo? Well, we found him *here*, at Neptune's Net. He's the chef."

Travis stared at her. "Manuelo?"

Chloe nodded. "He doesn't know we're here yet, I hope. When we ask him to come home, we want him to be way too surprised to say no."

Travis looked down at his plate, then back at Chloe. "I don't get it," he said. "I thought this was a date, not a reunion with your housekeeper. I mean, this is so stupid."

Chloe leaned close to Travis so no one else would hear her. "Stupid?" she repeated. "Maybe to you it's stupid, but Manuelo is part of my family. And my family is very important to me."

"What about me?" Travis replied. "I thought I was important to you. I mean, all this family stuff is totally boring."

Chloe thought about it. Travis *was* important to her—until now. Right now she thought he was selfish. He didn't care about her. He cared only about himself!

"Look, Travis, if you're bored, why don't you leave? I've got somebody much more important to talk to!" Chloe pushed back her chair and jumped to her feet. "I can't wait a second longer," she said to the others. "Let's go see Manuelo now!"

chapter
thirteen

Riley stood up quickly. "I guess it's show time," she said. "Come on, everybody!"

With her parents and Alex following her, Riley hurried across the dining room. Chloe was waiting at the kitchen door. "Ready?" she asked.

Riley nodded. "Let's do it."

Chloe pushed open the swinging door, and the Carlson family burst into the kitchen.

Riley glanced around. The place was hot, noisy, and busy. Pans clattered, food sizzled and steamed, cooks rushed back and forth between huge ranges and gleaming steel counters.

Riley grinned. There was Manuelo, stirring something in a saucepan. She was so glad to see him. "Manuelo!" she cried.

Manuelo had just lifted the spoon to his mouth. When he heard Riley, he froze.

"Hi, Manuelo!" Chloe called out.

"Surprise!" Jake and Macy shouted.

For a split second, Manuelo simply stared at them. But then a huge smile broke over his face. Dropping the spoon onto the counter, he sped across the kitchen floor with his arms open wide. "I am so happy to see you!" he cried.

Riley and Chloe hugged him. Macy gave him a kiss. Jake shook his hand and slapped him on the back.

"Manuelo, we're really sorry for hurting your feelings!" Riley exclaimed.

"We all feel terrible about it," Macy told him.

Jake nodded. "You had every right to be angry."

Before Manuelo could say anything, the door swung open and a waiter rushed in. Behind him was Larry, a frantic expression on his face. "Manuelo, I saw them coming in here, but I couldn't get to them in time to stop them," he declared. "And I just want you to know that I'm not the one who told them where you were. Your secret was safe with me."

"Then how did you find me?" Manuelo asked the Carlsons.

"We followed Larry," Chloe explained. "He led us straight to you."

"You *followed* me?" Larry asked indignantly. "That's, like, really sneaky!"

"Relax, Larry," Manuelo said. "I'm glad they found me. I've missed them."

"We missed you, too," Macy told him.

"So will you come home?" Riley asked. "Please? We'll never take you for granted again."

Manuelo frowned. "Never?"

"Okay, we'll try never do it again," Riley promised.

"Fair enough." Manuelo grinned. "Of course I will come home!"

Riley and Chloe hugged him again. "Where have you been staying?" Riley asked. "I mean, did you get an apartment or something?"

Manuelo shook his head. "I've been sleeping here, on a couch in the office," he said. "I was only filling in for a week, while the regular chef was on vacation. After that, I didn't know what I was going to do."

"Hey, this is working out great, isn't it?" Larry said. "I'm not in trouble, and everybody's happy. Except Travis," he added.

"Where *is* Travis?" Riley asked.

"He left a couple of minutes ago," Larry said. "And I hate to tell you, Chloe, but he wasn't smiling."

"What happened?" Riley asked, pulling her sister aside.

Chloe sighed. "It's a long story. Let's just say he wasn't boyfriend material."

Speaking of boyfriends, Riley thought. She glanced at Alex, who was talking to Jake and Macy. Then she edged closer to Manuelo. "Manuelo," she murmured, "I need your advice."

• • •

At school on Monday, Riley lingered outside the cafeteria, ready to put Manuelo's plan into action.

If it worked, she might be rid of Willow Sweet for good.

But if it failed…

[Riley: I'm not going to think about that. I'm going to keep telling myself that Manuelo was right about everything else. Why shouldn't he be right about this?]

Riley checked the time. Unfortunately, Alex and Willow had the same lunch period. They should be here any second. And they'd be together, of course. Willow would make sure of that.

"You have to be convincing," Manuelo had told her when he suggested the plan. "Both Alex and this Willow person must believe every word you say. Be prepared to act your heart out."

Riley glanced down the hall. There they were! She took a deep breath and watched.

Willow spotted her first. And just as Riley thought she would, Willow smirked. Then she said something to Alex, laughed, and slung an arm around his shoulders.

[Riley: Okay. Here goes!]

Riley stepped forward. "Hi, you guys."

Alex looked surprised to see her. "Hey, Riley!"

Willow's smirk turned into a smile. "I didn't know you had lunch now," she said. "Did you switch or something?"

Riley shook her head. "I was waiting for you two," she told them. "Could we talk for a minute?"

"Sure," Alex said.

Willow nodded. Her arm wasn't around Alex's shoulders anymore, but she was standing very close to him.

Riley took another deep breath. "I just wanted to apologize again about what happened the other day. You know, when I accused Willow of trying to get you back," she said to Alex.

Alex began to look uneasy.

"What I want to say is that you were right—I was jealous," Riley confessed. That was the true part. Now for the rest of it. "Anyway, I've been thinking about it a lot. And I realized that you and Willow are the perfect couple. I mean, I didn't want to admit it, but you really belong together!"

Willow's smirk was back, but Alex didn't seem to notice. He was staring at Riley, and the horrible thing was, she couldn't tell what he was thinking. Was this plan going to backfire?

You can't stop now, she told herself. It's too late. Just finish it and see what happens.

"So here's the deal. I wish things were different, but I know I can't change them," Riley said, trying to sound as convincing as possible. "So I'm not going to try." She paused. "I think you guys should get back together."

[**Riley**: There. I did it. I made the speech, and
now I'll have to live with what happens next.]

Willow sighed. "Riley, that is so nice of you! Actually,
I have a confession, too," she added, turning to Alex.
"Riley was right."

Alex blinked, confused. "About what?"

"Well, it would be so awesome if we got back
together," Willow said. "I mean, we *are* perfect together,
aren't we?"

Yes! Riley thought. Willow fell into the trap! But
what about Alex? What's *he* going to say? Riley's heart
pounded as she glanced at him.

Alex was staring at Willow.

Riley held her breath.

"Willow, listen," Alex said gently. "Maybe we used to
be perfect together, but we're not anymore."

Riley let out her breath.

"We're friends," Alex went on. "And I really like you,
but Riley's my girlfriend now." He turned to Riley. "Right?"

Thank you, Manuelo! Riley said silently.

Then she smiled at Alex. She didn't even bother to
look at Willow. "Right."

"You mean Willow didn't say a single word?" Chloe
asked Riley at home that night.

"Maybe she did, but I wasn't listening," Riley said.
"All I know is, she went into the cafeteria alone, and Alex
and I took a walk around the quad."

Riley grinned at Manuelo, who was tying a purple ribbon around Pepper's neck again. The whole family, plus Larry, was in the living room, getting ready for the new family portrait. The photographer was booked, so they'd recruited Larry to take the picture.

"I was so nervous," Riley went on. "But Manuelo's plan was perfect."

"Too bad I didn't ask his advice about Travis," Chloe said.

"I agree," Manuelo said. "Consult me next time, Chloe."

"I definitely will," Chloe promised.

"How come you're not more upset about Travis?" Riley asked her. "You thought he was so cool."

"I guess 'cool' isn't enough," Chloe said. "Anyway, now that I'm not wasting my time chasing him, I can find somebody else."

Larry looked up from the camera. "Okay, I think I've got it figured out," he announced. "Everybody get ready."

They all took their places on the couch again. This time Manuelo sat in the middle, with Pepper on his lap. Riley and Chloe sat on either side of him, while Jake and Macy perched on the arms of the sofa.

"Let's see..." Larry muttered, fiddling with the camera's settings.

Riley glanced at Manuelo. "Psst! Manuelo," she said, trying not to move her lips. "Want some advice? Just between us?"

He glanced at her out of the corner of his eye. "Of course, Riley. What is it? Is my tie crooked? My hair messed up?"

Riley shook her head. "Just say *cheese!*"

He did. So did everyone else.

Larry snapped the picture.

And the Carlson family portrait was finally complete.

mary-kate olsen **ashley** olsen

so little time

Chloe
and Riley's

SCRAPBOOK

Here's a sneak peek at

**A special
three-part series.**

BOOK 2

Wishes and Dreams

We turned the corner at the end of the hall—and nearly crashed into Rachel Adams.

"Hey, Mary-Kate. Hi, Ashley. I got your e-mail invitation—thanks!" she said.

"You're welcome," I told her with a smile. "Do you think you can make it to our party?"

"I'll be there for sure—and I *love* that the girls are inviting the guys. I'm asking tons of boys, so we should have enough to dance with and—"

I turned and looked at Ashley, whose face had gone completely pale. "Um, did you just say you're inviting *tons* of boys?" I asked Rachel. "You were only supposed to invite one."

Rachel looked at me with a confused expression. "Well, your e-mail said to invite *guys*. Plural," she explained. "So I thought I'd invite the guys' basketball team. Then I asked my older brother if he'd come along and bring a couple of his friends, because some of them are really cute."

"Yeah, um, that sounds great!" Ashley said. She started pulling me away. "I'm sorry, Rachel, but we have to run now. See you later!"

Ashley and I raced down the hall. I knew where we were headed. We had to get to the computer lab to check out the e-mail we sent.

"We didn't," I said as we ran.

"We couldn't have," Ashley agreed. We rushed into the lab and grabbed a seat at one of the terminals. Ashley signed on to our e-mail account in record time. She pulled up our "Sent Mail."

Suddenly, there it was on the screen: our latest e-mail update about our sweet sixteen party. Ashley ran her finger along the message until she got to the important line.

"Please invite the guys of your choice," she read.

"Rachel was right! It's *guys*—plural!" I wailed.

Several heads popped up from behind computer monitors as people strained to see what was going on.

"Mary-Kate," Ashley whispered, "the entire school is going to come to our party now. The entire city! We can't have a party for all of those people. What are we going to do?"

BE A CHARACTER IN A MARY-KATE AND ASHLEY BOOK SWEEPSTAKES!

so little time

IT COULD BE YOU!

COMPLETE THIS ENTRY FORM:

ENTER

BE A CHARACTER IN A MARY-KATE AND ASHLEY BOOK SWEEPSTAKES!

No purchase necessary. See details on back.

Name: _____

Address: _____

City: _____ State: _____ Zip: _____

Phone: _____ Age: _____

Mail to: **BE A CHARACTER IN A MARY-KATE AND ASHLEY BOOK SWEEPSTAKES**
C/O HarperEntertainment
Attention: Children's Marketing Department
10 East 53rd Street, New York, NY 10022

SO LITTLE TIME
Be a Character in a Mary-Kate and Ashley Book Sweepstakes

OFFICIAL RULES:

1. No purchase necessary.

2. To enter complete the official entry form or hand print your name, address, age, and phone number along with the words "SO LITTLE TIME Be a Character in a Mary-Kate and Ashley Book Sweepstakes" on a 3" x 5" card and mail to: SO LITTLE TIME Be a Character in a Mary-Kate and Ashley Book Sweepstakes, c/o HarperEntertainment, Attn: Children's Marketing Department, 10 East 53rd Street, New York, NY 10022. Entries must be received by **December 31, 2002**. Enter as often as you wish, but each entry must be mailed separately. One entry per envelope. Partially completed, illegible, or mechanically reproduced entries will not be accepted. Sponsors are not responsible for lost, late, mutilated, illegible, stolen, postage due, incomplete, or misdirected entries. All entries become the property of Dualstar Entertainment Group, Inc., and will not be returned.

3. Sweepstakes open to all legal residents of the United States, (excluding Colorado and Rhode Island), who are between the ages of five and fifteen on December 31, 2002, excluding employees and immediate family members of HarperCollins Publishers, Inc. ("HarperCollins"), Parachute Properties and Parachute Press, Inc., and their respective subsidiaries and affiliates, officers, directors, shareholders, employees, agents, attorneys, and other representatives (individually and collectively "Parachute"), Dualstar Entertainment Group, Inc., and its subsidiaries and affiliates, officers, directors, shareholders, employees, agents, attorneys, and other representatives (individually and collectively "Dualstar"), and their respective parent companies, affiliates, subsidiaries, advertising, promotion and fulfillment agencies, and the persons with whom each of the above are domiciled. Offer void where prohibited or restricted by law.

4. Odds of winning depend on the total number of entries received. Approximately 225,000 sweepstakes announcements published. Prize will be awarded. Winner will be randomly drawn on or about January 15, 2003, by HarperEntertainment, whose decisions are final. Potential winner will be notified by mail and will be required to sign and return an affidavit of eligibility and release of liability within 14 days of notification. Prizes won by minors will be awarded to parent or legal guardian who must sign and return all required legal documents. By acceptance of prize, winner consents to the use of his or her name, photograph, likeness, and personal information by HarperCollins, Parachute, Dualstar, and for publicity purposes without further compensation except where prohibited.

5. One (1) **Grand Prize Winner** will have his or her name in a Mary-Kate and Ashley book, as a character; and receive an autographed copy of the book in which the winner's name appears. HarperCollins, Parachute and Dualstar reserve the right to substitute another prize of equal or greater value in the event that the winner is unable to receive the prize for any reason. Approximate retail value: $4.50. **Winner will not be permitted to review book prior to publication.**

6. Only one prize will be awarded per individual, family, or household. Prizes are non-transferable and cannot be sold or redeemed for cash. No cash substitute is available. Any federal, state, or local taxes are the responsibility of the winner. Sponsor may substitute prize of equal or greater value, if necessary, due to availability.

7. Additional terms: By participating, entrants agree a) to the official rules and decisions of the judges, which will be final in all respects; and to waive any claim to ambiguity of the official rules and b) to release, discharge, and hold harmless HarperCollins, Parachute, Dualstar, and their affiliates, subsidiaries, and advertising and promotion agencies from and against any and all liability or damages associated with acceptance, use, or misuse of any prize received in this sweepstakes.

8. Any dispute arising from this Sweepstakes will be determined according to the laws of the State of New York, without reference to its conflict of law principles, and the entrants consent to the personal jurisdiction of the State and Federal courts located in New York County and agree that such courts have exclusive jurisdiction over all such disputes.

9. To obtain the name of the winners, please send your request and a self-addressed stamped envelope (excluding residents of Vermont and Washington) to: SO LITTLE TIME Be a Character in a Mary-Kate and Ashley Book Sweepstakes, c/o HarperEntertainment, Attn: Children's Marketing Department, 10 East 53rd Street, New York, NY 10022 by February 1, 2003. Sweepstakes Sponsor: HarperCollins Publishers, Inc.

The Ultimate Fa...

mary-kate

Don't miss

The New Adventures of MARY-KATE & ASHLEY™

- ❑ The Case Of The Great Elephant Escape
- ❑ The Case Of The Summer Camp Caper
- ❑ The Case Of The Surfing Secret
- ❑ The Case Of The Green Ghost
- ❑ The Case Of The Big Scare Mountain Mystery
- ❑ The Case Of The Slam Dunk Mystery
- ❑ The Case Of The Rock Star's Secret
- ❑ The Case Of The Cheerleading Camp Mystery
- ❑ The Case Of The Flying Phantom
- ❑ The Case Of The Creepy Castle

- ❑ The Case Of The Golden Slipper
- ❑ The Case Of The Flapper 'Napper
- ❑ The Case Of The High Seas Secret
- ❑ The Case Of The Logical I Ranch
- ❑ The Case Of The Dog Camp Mystery
- ❑ The Case Of The Screaming Scarecrow
- ❑ The Case Of The Jingle Bell Jinx
- ❑ The Case Of The Game Show Mystery
- ❑ The Case Of The Mall Mystery
- ❑ The Case Of The Weird Science Mystery
- ❑ The Case Of Camp Crooked Lake

Starring in

- ❑ Switching Goals
- ❑ Our Lips Are Sealed
- ❑ Winning London
- ❑ School Dance Party
- ❑ Holiday in the Sun

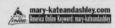

  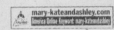